Hold You Down: Ahmad and Pia

Dominique Thomas

Hold You Down: Ahmad and Pia

Published by Shan Presents

www.shanpresents.com

Table of Contents

Chapter One

Pia
My Younger Years

"This is our new home," my dad said, looking from me to my brothers. I nodded, gazing around the huge house that was twice the size of our last home. My dad was always moving us around. Sometimes, we stayed with our mom, Portia, when she decided to come get us, but it was never longer than a few days.

My brothers Pablo and Primero, whom we called Primo, walked around while I stood in the middle of the floor looking at my dad. He seemed so much bigger than my brothers and I. I couldn't put into words how much I loved him.

"Princess, I'm going to take you all over to our friend's home. Go get your shoes," he said, ruffling my hair.

I rushed off as fast as I could and grabbed my Mary Janes. My father chose to dress me like I was a princess, only having his stylist get me dresses and flat shoes with bows on them and stuff like that. I only had five pairs of jeans in my wardrobe, with closets full of dresses. I used to hate it, but I was used to it now.

I fixed my hair in two very long pigtails and grabbed my small purse, throwing it over my shoulder like a crossbody bag. I glanced at myself in the mirror and smiled. I was average height, I guess, for a twelve-year-old. I had pale skin that looked really cute in the summer with a tan along with a small, round face and long, wavy brown hair. What I did like about myself were my thick eyebrows and my long eyelashes. Portia always said they were so pretty on me.

"Come on, Princess!" my dad yelled, getting my attention.

I smiled at myself before rushing off. I met my dad in the hallway, and he grabbed my hand before leading me out of our new home and into one of his shiny black cars that looked like something you would see in the future. As my dad pulled away from the house, I looked out of the window.

"Pia, do you miss your mother?"

I shrugged. Did I miss Portia? I mean sometimes I did, then sometimes I didn't. She could be a lot to deal with at times.

"Sometimes," I replied quietly. My dad sighed almost like my answer saddened him.

"She loves you, Pia, she is just dealing with a lot right now," he said, lying for her. He'd been telling us that for years, but whenever I turned on a video there, Portia was having the time of her life. She could do a video, but she couldn't visit us? Didn't seem like she was going through anything to me.

"I know," I said, rolling my eyes.

"Well, she's coming into town next week so you will get to see her then," he said excitedly. His eagerness to see her must have been on his own behalf because he knew that Portia wasn't coming to town to visit my brothers or me.

After turning down a few blocks, we arrived at a beautiful home. We parked in the driveway and got out as a fewout front, talking. My dad walked over to them, and I saw they were the same men I'd met at a beautiful cabin, deep the woods. I liked how nice they were to my brothers and me, so I waved at them while staying by my dad's side. We all walked in and there he was, sitting on the bottom step with a DS in his hand. I wasn't sure what it was, but my stomach felt funny whenever he was around. His hazel eyes peered at me, and his cute, light brown-skinned face frowned while I smiled back at him, too happy to be in his presence. This was what we always did when we saw one another.

"Ugh, really dad damn," he huffed, and his father Ameer slapped him in the back of his head while my dad and the other men chuckled.

"Don't start, Ahmad. Take Pia to the park while the grown folks talk," his dad told him in a stern tone.

Ahmad rolled his pretty hazel eyes and slowly stood. He was much taller than me and for him to only be twelve, he was also starting to get a small mustache. He was wearing basketball shorts with a black beater and Jordan slides. He put his DS in his pocket and walked over to me. I opened my mouth to speak to him, and he quickly shook his head, hushing me. I closed my mouth and anticipated what he would say.

"Let's go," he mumbled, grabbing my hand.

"Princess, no rough playing and stay close to Ahmad," my dad said as we exited the house.

"Okay, Daddy!" I yelled while squeezing Ahmad's hand tightly. The minute we were outside, he let my hand go.

"Damn, you got my shit on lock. Chill out," he complained. I stared at him as we walked down his driveway. "I mean what the fuck I look like? I already have to watch my bad ass sisters, now they got me babysitting yo' ass. This some straight upbullshit," he said angrily.

I swear he was the only twelve year old I knew that cursed like they were grown. I giggled because he was just too funny to me and we stopped walking. Ahmad's eyes gave me a slow, deliberate once-over that made my cheeks darken. He was always so serious. He acted as if he was a grown man already.

"Look, don't talk to none of these niggasthat's around here. Okay?"

I nodded, and he shook his head.

"No, say okay, Pia. I need for you to know these dudes ain't nothing but games. Do you understand, Pia?"

I rolled my eyes and placed my hands on my small hips. "I said okay, Ahmad. Dang."

Ahmad looked at me and chuckled.

"Aye, that attitude is not cute. You not a princess to me so watch how you talk to me with your Sponge Bob Square Pants shaped ass," he said and swaggered away.

"Sponge Bob?" I frowned, walking behind him.

"Yeah, you got a fucked up shape already, Pia. That's not a good look, ma," he yelled over his shoulder before laughing.

"Whatever," I huffed, getting irritated with him. I followed Ahmad to another big house, and we walked around to the backyard. Three cute boys stood on this large basketball court shooting hoops while two girls around my age sat down on the grass watching them. Ahmad took off his beater and handed it to me along with his DS and his cell phone. He leaned towards me, and I smiled thinking he was about to kiss me. I even licked my lips. He grabbed some lint from my hair and laughed.

"Look, when you chilling with me you gotta stay fly. You looking way too uptight with that frizzy ass hair. Do better, Pia," he said and walked away.

Frizzy? I was in between my wash days, but still I looked cute. I watched him jog onto the court with his friends.

"So you know Ahmad?" one of the girls asked me as I sat down by them.

I looked at both girls and saw that they were beautiful and a lot thicker than me.

"Yes, I do," I said, and the girl with slanted brown eyes smacked her lips. I'd had seen her before, and she was acting very stuck up that last time. I wasn't sure what her problem was. My mom told me that because I was pretty, girls would always want to fight me. I didn't believe that, though. At my old school, I had a lot of friends. However, I wasn't sure how it would be at my new one.

"Well, he kissed me all over my stomach last night, so you two must not be too close," she said, making the girl next to her laugh.

"Rowan, leave that girl alone. We all know Ahmad is your *boyfriend*," her friend said.

Rowan smirked and started staring at me. Her gaze was intense, she looked at everything I had on without embarrassment.

"How old are you? You dress like my little sister with that big ass dress on and them Mary Janes. Ugh, and those pigtails, you need a fucking makeover with your homely looking ass," she said, and they both cracked laughing at me.

My eyes watered at her scrutiny of my look. I had grown to like my dresses, and my shoes were special to me. The designer himself had signed the bottom of them. I got up and walked closer to the court while they laughed harder. I didn't want to sit and be the butt of their jokes. Ahmad glanced over at me while holding the ball and he stopped smiling. His good mood seemed to be instantly gone as he made his way over to me.

"What's wrong, Ugly?" he asked out of concern. I shook my head, and he looked past me and at the girls who sat on the grass. He shook his head and wiped away one of my tears that had somehow escaped from my eye.

"Fuck them, girls. They jealous and if you let them see you crying, then you playing into their game. Give me my shirt," he said, and I quickly handed him his shirt. He slipped it on and tossed his ball at his friend who I knew was named Shawn, but everybody called him Shyy. He was Ahmad's best friend. Whatever Ahmad did, he did it too. He took the ball and shook his head.

"Damn so for Pia you drop everything, huh? I see you, playa," he joked.

Ahmad chuckled but chose not to reply. However, Rowan voiced her opinion immediately.

"Ahmad, who is she? You said you liked me. That I was your girlfriend," she said standing up.

Ahmad grabbed my hand, and we walked past Rowan and her friend. She grabbed his arm, and he looked back at her.

"Rowan, I'll call you later," he said before pulling his arm away.

I glanced back at her, and she rolled her eyes at me before mouthing "stupid bitch." I shook my head and walked with Ahmad away from the house. He took us to a park nearby, and I got on the swing. He pushed me for a few minutes before we decided to lay on the grass by the lake which he and all of his neighbors had access to.

"So where yo' moms at Ugly?"

I shook my head at his ignorance, still smiling. We were both on our back and for some reason holding hands. I mean I guess it just felt right.

"She's in Chicago. She *models*. Where is your mother?"

"Dead," he said and cleared his throat. "I remember her, though. When she was alive, she wasn't that nice to me. I remember always wishing she would do stuff with me. It was like she was always too busy for me and shit," he replied, and man did I know that feeling.

"Well, that is how my mom is now. My dad takes care of my brothers and me because Portia doesn't have time to raise us properly. She's very selfish."

"Damn," he said, and we sort of both got lost in our thoughts.

"Well you ugly as hell, you skinny and you dress like Matilda, so I don't like you, but we can be best friends. Being my best friend means you can't date any boy I know because that's disrespectful to me. Boys lie anyway, so why even waste your time," he said. I thought about Portia and all of the nasty things I had witnessed her doing with boys. It sounded good to me.

"So, I won't have to kiss anybody or anything like that?" I asked, just to make sure.

"Yeah! I mean girls that do that stuff is nasty anyway. You're too good for that Ugly," he replied making me smile.

"Okay hold up," he said letting my hand go. He pulled a pocket knife out of his shoe, and I started to laugh. Who walked around with pocket knives on them?

"I saw this shit in a movie. This how the gangsters do it "P"," he said and grabbed my finger. My heart was pounding in my chest as he pricked my finger then his. He pushed his bloody finger against mine and looked me in the eyes.

"Best friends for life," he said, and we both laughed.

Chapter Two

Pia

Present day

"Man, we were having so much fun at Rowan's party. Ahmad was in the basement with her ass all night, too!" Shyy said all animated, like only he could as we walked out of the school.

Zaria looked over at me and gave me a knowing look before shaking her head. I knew this would only add fuel to her fire. She for some reason hated Ahmad.

"So Ahmad is seeing Rowan again?" she asked Shyy on the sly to see what he would say.

He watched some girl pass by us, and he winked at her. He was always trying to talk to some damn body. The girl blushed, and he looked back at Zaria.

"Hell yeah. They gone always be together in some kind of way. You know he was her first and shit," he said before looking my way. Shyy looked me in the eyes, and he stopped smiling. "Well not like how you and Ahmad are, though. I mean you and him are…y'all just…"

"Pia! Wait up!" Ahmad yelled running up to us. He threw his arm over my shoulder, and I tried to push him away. I didn't want him touching me. Ahmad threw his arm back over my shoulder again and frowned leering at me. "What's wrong with you?"

I looked at Shyy, and he quickly walked away from us and went to his Range Rover. Zaria threw her angry eyes Ahmad's way and sucked her teeth.

"So you tell us not to go to Rowan's party so that you could be there fucking her all night?" she asked saying pretty much what I was thinking. Rowan and I weren't cool, but that party had been talked about for months, and the reason I didn't go was because Ahmad asked me not to, claiming he wasn't going.

Ahmad moved his arm from away from my shoulder and grabbed my hand. Zaria pulled out her car keys while mumbling stuff up under her breath. He ignored her and looked at me.

"Come with me. We need to talk," he said staring down at me. Zaria looked from me to him and laughed.

"Pia, come on. He obviously is back with her even after she fucked his friend on the basketball team. Fuck him," she said, opening her car door. Ahmad turned his angry hazel eyes her way.

"You talk too fucking much, Zaria. Take your tarter smelling ass home. Bitch need to be in a fucking tub anyway. We all know that's your dirty ass pussy funking up the math class and shit," he said, making embarrassment wash over her face.

"Nigga what? You are so full of shit! You act like a baby anytime Pia gets a guy friend that she like yet you fuck every girl in the damn school. How that work?"

Ahmad chuckled and pulled me to his side wrapping his arm around my waist.

"Look Pia is my best friend. I don't gotta explain shit to you," he said and pulled me away. I was used to them fighting, so I chose to stay out of it. As long as they were keeping their hands to themselves, I was minding my own business.

Ahmad and I walked to his old-school, tricked-out matte black Grand National andwe both got in. While he put his backpack in the backseat, Rowan walked by his car with her flock of groupies. Rowan was now the head cheerleader and the one girl every guy in the school wanted to sleep with. She was dressing like Portia, which was what I classified as whore gear. I still wore my dresses and Mary Janes, but I had upgraded to jeans as well with cardigans and Polos. Zaria said I dressed like I stepped off of a Ralph Lauren ad. I wasn't sure about that. I just like to look polished and neat. I never wanted a boy to approach me because I had my ass or titties hanging out.

"On some real shit, hanging with that hoe is going to get you into something," he said as he pulled off not paying Rowan any attention, although she was staring at him so damn hard she nearly tripped over her feet.

I rolled my eyes. He was bossy as ever trying to delegate what I did and didn't do.

"Whatever Ahmad, I could say the same thing to you. Rowan is a hoe, yet you hang out with her and was even her boyfriend a few months ago," I told him and shook my head at the thought of him being with her. He had openly been her man a few months prior, and I didn't talk to him the whole time. Needless to say, that relationship didn't last long.

"Yeah, okay. So what you doing tonight?"

I stared out of the window. Just knowing he'd spent his time this weekend fucking Rowan hurt me. We weren't together, but he very much belonged to me. She wanted him because he was popular. Because he was a Matin. His family was like Detroit royalty. His father and uncles had DVDs out about the things they did when they were younger. All of the boys in school admired Ahmad, and all of the girls wanted him. Rowan didn't love him like I did and she never would. She didn't even know the real him. How he hated scary movies or how he had bad ass allergies and loved to watch the Lion King with his sisters. She never got to see that side of him, and I know because I was always around him. The only time we spent apart since we were twelve was at night and on the weekends when I went to Chicago to visit Portia. So that left her with just enough time to get fucked by him, and that's it.

"I don't know," I mumbled in a bad mood.

Ahmad touched my hair and yanked on the end of it. He knew I hated when he did that yet he still did it. He was so damn irritating sometimes.

"Then you coming home with me. Call your pops. I need you to help me with my work while I babysit my bad ass sisters," he told me versus asking me.

I groaned and rolled my eyes. I loved Ahmad's sisters. Really, his family in general. At one point my dad was messing with his aunt, and that didn't end well which resulted in my dad no longer being cool with Ahmad's people. They still treated me nice, however. I appreciated them for that because I would have gone crazy if they would have tried to pull Ahmad and me apart. He worked my nerves daily, but he was my everything.

"Whatever, Ahmad."

"*Whatever, Ahmad,*" he mimicked me and cut on his radio.

I texted my dad and told him I would be home later while Ahmad drove to his home. He still stayed in this a huge mansion that I had grown to love. He pulled into his driveway and parked near the front door. I looked over at him, and he smiled at me. Man, I loved his smiles because I always got to see his nice teeth. For some reason, I loved guys with nice teeth.

"Ahmad, mama is gonna get you," I told him looking at the driveway, seeing how we were parked near the door. He chuckled and opened his door.

"Pia, you so damn scared of my moms. My legs hurt like a motherfucka. She can't talk shit about me parking here today," he said grabbing his book bag.

"Okay," I said laughing as I got out of the car. Before Ahmad could get fully around his car, his momma, Sophie was stepping out of the house in a sexy body hugging dress that showed off all of her curves. My face lit up when I saw her.

"Hey, Ma!" I yelled meeting her on the steps. Sophie hugged me and rubbed my back. She looked at me and smiled. She was the only woman I had ever called mom, and that meant something to me.

"Hi daughter, you look beautiful as always. Can you tell my son to move that fucking car before I whoop his extra tall ass?" she asked me smiling. I giggled. This was why I loved coming over here.

"Ahmad, Ma said can you move that fucking car before she whoops your extra tall ass?" I asked him.

"Thanks, Pia," Sophie said staring at Ahmad.

Ahmad groaned, and I stared back at him. His hazel eyes were narrowed, but he knew not to talk shit. He pouted and made this sexy, adorable face that always got him what he wanted. Damn, I really did love him.

"Ma…really? Why does the driveway go by the door if we can't park here?" he asked which kind of made sense I guess.

"Move the car Ahmad," she said again with finality in her voice, and together we walked away while he begrudgingly moved his car. I followed Sophie into the house and took my shoes off at the door. Her two girls ran up to me smiling and giggling. Soraya and Ameerah were just too cute for their own good. I bent down and gave both of my beautiful girls a hug. Soraya was the oldest, and I swear a little diva in the making.

"Hey, girls, y'all ready to have some fun?"

They both nodded as Ahmad stepped into the house.

"Ma, Soraya straight up broke my headphones and shit. Did she get whooped for that, though? Y'all be letting this girl get away with murder," he complained.

Soraya giggled while Sophie glared at Ahmad. She put her hands on her hips and gave him that look that immediately calmed his attitude down. He walked over to her and looked down into her eyes. What was funny was that over the years he had gotten taller than both of us. He had to be at least six-three now and he was still freaking growing.

"Ma, you know I'm your favorite Matin man," he said making her blush. He kissed her cheek and pulled her into a hug making her laugh. Ahmad let her go, and she glanced over at me.

"I don't know how you deal with this boy Pia," she said still smiling. Hell, I didn't know how I dealt with him either.

"Ma, he looks at me with them eyes and I just forgive him," I told her truthfully.

"Them eyes get 'em every time," Ameer, Ahmad's dad said stepping into the walkway wearing a custom-made suit. I looked up at him smiling He was so handsome and smelled so good it made you want to sniff him a few times just to say *hmmm*. It was obvious Ahmad got his eyes and his looks from him. Ameer pulled Sophie into a hug and whispered something in her ear before turning his attention to me. "You good, Pia?"

"Yes, I am," I replied.

"She good Pops, with her old water headed ass…I mean butt," Ahmad said, immediately correcting himself. Ahmad walked over to me and put me in a headlock. The girls started hitting on him and jumping on his leg while I tried to break free. He played too damn much.

"Stop, Ahmad! My hair!" I yelled, not wanting my hair to tangle up.

"Ahmad, leave that girl alone. You always picking on my baby," Sophie said, and he let me go. Sophie and Ameer looked at both of us with these small smiles on their face.

"Well, we going to this event for my real estate company so we will be out late. You two know the rules. Nobody in the house while we're gone. So no Shyy, Ahmad. Pia make sure the girls take baths and are in bed by eight," Ameer said to the both of us.

"Okay, got it," I said while Ahmad played with Ameerah. I'm sure he wasn't listening. His ass is always in his own world.

"Ahmad, let me talk to you right quick," Ameer said walking away. Ahmad went after

him while Sophie put on another coat of gloss. I loved to watch her prep for when they went somewhere fancy because she always looked gorgeous. I would even sit in the room with her sometimes and watch her do her hair.

"Ma, how do you put on makeup?"

Sophie looked at me.

"It's easy, but you don't need any, Pia. You're beautiful just the way you are, baby. We'll go to the mall this weekend and grab you some starter stuff. Nothing major because it might break your face out," she replied as Ameer and Ahmad walked back into the room. Sophie kissed the girls then Ahmad and me before they left out of the house. I walked to the door and set the alarm. I was one of the few people outside of Ahmad's immediate family that knew the alarm code. Sophie had given it to me last year, and I felt so honored when she did. It was like I was one of them.

The girls and I fell into our regular routine of playing with dolls and me painting their nails. Soraya liked for me to help her dress all of her baby dolls and then go through her purse collection. Ahmad played his video game with Shyy online while I helped them with their homework and made tacos to eat for dinner. I knew his parents had left money for pizza, but the ground turkey was already unthawed, so I took advantage of it.

Eight o'clock soon rolled around, and I was tucking the girls into bed after their baths. They were fed, clean, and tired, which was a good thing. I kissed both of them and found Ahmad in his bed now playing the game on his flat screen instead of in the basement. Ahmad's bedroom was most definitely a boy's room. He had a few pics of some video vixen that I hated, and other than that he had his basketball trophies on the back wall shelves. His bed was a four poster king size bed. I took off my cardigan and laid down on my back. My cell started to ring as I pulled it out of my pocket.

My dad was out of town, and my brothers were hanging out in the streets, so I knew I had at least three more hours with Ahmad. I peeked at the screen and smiled. *This girl.*

"Hello."

"Pia! Why did I just talk to Justin and he said that Xerius likes you," Zaria said excitedly. I couldn't stop myself from smiling. I was not expecting her to say that. Xerius was cool with Ahmad, and all of his friends knew not to even come at me like that, so for him to tell Justin he liked me came as a shock.

"Are you sure?"

"Yeah! I just talked to Justin and Xerius was in the background talking about how sexy you are with your preppy look you be working. He said all of the boys be checking for you out, but Ahmad be hating and threatening to beat niggas up for even speaking your name," she replied. I laughed because that sounded like something his crazy ass would do.

Xerius was cute, but I wasn't interested in him in that kind of way.

"Girl, ain't nobody thinking about Xerius," I said, and Ahmad looked back at me.

I broke his gaze and soon he was coming towards me with a deep scowl on his face. He grabbed my phone and started arguing with Zaria.

"See, this why I don't like yo ass. You always on this hoe shit. Look, Pia and me studying you gotta call her back," he said and ended the call. I snatched my phone away from him and glared at him like he was crazy.

"Stop fucking doing that. You don't pay my phone bill, Ahmad. I can talk to Zaria if I want to," I said and shoved the shit out of his arm. At one point in time, I had been so sweet but being around Ahmad had toughened me up. I now cursed like a sailor and had hit him more than I liked to admit. It was just something about him. He was the only person that could piss me off to the point where I had to lay hands on him. I knew it wasn't right, so I was trying to change that.

Ahmad smirked before pushing me back hard as hell. I had to catch myself from falling off of the bed. He laughed and licked his lips. He had this look in his eyes that told me he was up to something. He scooted over my way, and I put my hand up in the air while laughing.

"Stay your ass over there, Ahmad," I told him scooting back as far as I could. Shit, I was hanging halfway off of the bed. Ahmad shook his head and grabbed my leg. He pulled me to the center of the bed and somehow I ended up under him. He buried his head into my neck, and I laid on the bed nervously. This was the very reason why I didn't want a boyfriend. Ahmad had my mind all messed up.

"You know I'm fucking that nigga Xerius up, right?" he asked and buried his face into my neck. His soft full lips kissed me on the neck. I squirmed beneath him as his warm tongue slowly started to suck on my skin. I wish I could put into words how good it felt to have Ahmad suck on me, but I couldn't. What I did know was that I liked it.

"Ahmad…*stop*," I said breathlessly. He chuckled while pulling back. His hazel eyes were slightly closed as he looked down at me.

"What you like that nigga or something?"

I immediately shook my head. How did he come up with that?

"No, but I mean I don't have a boyfriend."

Ahmad pulled his bottom lip into his mouth and nodded his head. I rolled my eyes finding it comical how jealous he could be yet, I had to watch him date *everybody*.

"We'll see how much you like him when I crack that nigga's jaw," he said and kissed me on the lips this time. I pushed his shoulders because the last thing he needed to be doing was fighting and he chuckled against my mouth. He slowly slid his tongue into my mouth and we both moaned. Shit.

My eyes closed and I grabbed his shoulders to draw him closer to me. I opened my legs, and he started to grind his erection slowly against me. He was now in basketball shorts, and I was still in my jeans. His hand slid between our bodies, and he fumbled with the button of my jeans. My eyes shot open, and I pushed him back.

"No, my period is here," I lied. He stared at me for a moment.

"Stop lying. It comes at the end of the month. Usually, the eighteenth or the nineteenth because I know to be nice to you that week, and you always have me bring you sweets and shit. Come on let me touch it, Ugly," he said and smirked. I pouted while shaking my head.

"Stop calling me that Ahmad. I'm not twelve anymore."

Ahmad laughed as he slowly slid his hand into my jeans.

"I know and you the prettiest, ugly girl I have ever seen," he said as his long fingers found their way into my panties. He started to slowly massage my clitoris, and I whimpered. Each time I considered sticking a finger in myself, I felt bad. I mean Portia let men do this type of stuff to her and look at how they treated her. Trash got more respect out of them than she did.

"Ahmad…please stop…this is nasty," I told him.

Ahmad kissed me again while staring me in the eyes. After a few minutes, he pulled back and looked at me.

"With me, this is okay Pia. I would never treat you like that. Let me feel it..." he stuck his face into my neck. He started sucking on my earlobe as he whispered, "Please...I wanna make you cum," he said.

I grew wetter at his words. I closed my eyes with my heart beating rapidly. I slowly nodded, and he sighed with relief. His finger slowly slipped inside of me and I winced from the pain. He slowly added another finger and started to move them around. It was very uncomfortable and slightly painful. I pushed him back slightly, and he sat up. Our eyes connected and I was able to see the lust he had for me. He slipped my hand into his gym shorts and made me wrap my hand around it. Damn it was, velvety soft yet hard like a rock not to mention it was long as hell.

I slowly stroked him as we stared at one another. I grabbed some of his pre-cum that was falling from the head and used it to massage him. His eyes closed briefly as he moved his fingers faster inside of me. I arched my back loving the pleasure he was giving me. I had a jittery feeling in my stomach that I had never felt before. Shit, it kind of scared me.

"Damn, you so fucking wet and tight. I can't wait to get this, Pia. When you gone stop playing with me?" he asked, but no words could leave my mouth. I was stuck in between heaven and earth. My body was floating higher to heaven as he worked his magic. I tightened my grip on him, and as his body shuddered making cum shoot off into my hand, my body exploded releasing all over his fingers.

BAM! BAM! BAM!

"Ahmad, did Pia go home?"

Ahmad and I both jumped. He sat back, still breathing hard while I rubbed his cum off onto his comforter We quickly fixed ourselves and minutes later, his door was being pulled open. Ameer stood in the doorway with hooded red eyes. He looked at both of us, and a sly grin slid over his face.

"Lucky for you, your Momma is drunk and asleep. Go take Pia home," he said and left the room. Ahmad looked at me, and we both smiled. Us getting each other off was a first. He chuckled as he got out of the bed. I watched him lick the fingers that had been inside of me. I blushed and got myself together so that I could go home.

Chapter Three

Pia

"Then that bitch wanna act like she the shit when her momma is doing freak videos and shit. I heard she even got a porno out with some rappers. I swear this hoe is no different," Rowan whispered to someone behind me. I stared at her, and they both stared straight ahead with blank expressions on their faces as if they weren't throwing dirt on Portia's name. I was so irritated I could have killed her. This was a new low for her.

"If you got something to say at least be woman enough to say the shit to my face," I snapped at her.

"Pia! Come here," Ahmad said from across the room.

The teacher peered at me but didn't say anything. He was a sub and as long as we did our work he was cool. I gathered my books and stood up. As I walked by Rowan's desk, she stared me down but didn't say shit. She knew that talking to me in front of Ahmad would be a problem.

"Why you in here tripping? Arguing like a rat and shit, fuck them," he said as I sat down next to him. His group of friends who happened to be the varsity basketball players and a few football players surrounded us. I shrugged and put my head down on the desk. I was tired as hell. Ahmad scooted his desk closer to mine, and he draped his jacket over my shoulders. He had a game tonight, and I was going to miss it because I had to spend time with Portia. I loathed spending time with her.

"You gotta give me something before you go with her to the Chi," he whispered in my ear and then laid his head on my arm.

I smiled although I knew he couldn't see me.

"So who having a party tonight?" Shyy asked.

"Ahmad, ain't yo uncle renting out that suite for us?" another teammate asked him. I could feel him tense up against my arm.

"Yeah, but calm that shit down," he replied with an attitude.

"Well, I know I'm coming," Rowan said from the other side of the room. I glanced across at her. Rowan was beautiful, and that was what made me so angry. I wasn't a hater, but to see her beauty and know that some part of Ahmad liked it made me mad. She was thicker than I knew I would ever be and she seemed to have the biggest ass with large breast that never sagged. While I had a more toned body with hips and nice size butt, she was curvy like the girls in music videos. Her hair was usually in some high-end sew-in, and she always had on something provocative.

She smirked at me, as Ahmad touched my thigh. He and I were just friends, but we were so much more now. However, I didn't know how to approach that subject with him. Plus, he was having sex and had been for years. I was afraid of giving myself to him, and he knew that. I saw no reason to keep him from doing something he enjoyed, that was another reason why I hadn't asked him to make us official.

I put my head back down on the desk, and his hand went to my stomach. Today I was wearing high waist jeans, a white cami, and a striped cardigan. The jeans had my butt looking big as hell, and I had been getting compliments left and right. The best one coming from Ahmad. He said, 'I looked way less ugly than I usually do,' which in his words meant I was looked beautiful. That whole ugly thing was something only we still laughed at. Nobody got it, but it wasn't for them to understand. Ahmad and I didn't have to make sense to them, shit even if I told them they wouldn't get it.

"You smell so good Pia, and I'm hungry," he whined. I laughed, as he rubbed my stomach. "You see your boy?" he asked changing the subject. I rolled my eyes. Xerius hadn't come to school in a few days, and I was happy. Ahmad had been looking for him relentlessly since finding out he liked me.

"No, did you?"

Ahmad pinched my thigh hard as hell.

"Owe! Stop," I said and pushed him. Ahmad chuckled and grabbed my cheek. He started to pinch it, and then the sub cleared his throat. A few people laughed and even slapped

Ahmad on his back. They hyped up whatever he did even the stupid shit.

"Ugh. How old are we again?" Rowan's friend Karra said and made a gagging sound. Rowan and her groupies all laughed. I rolled my eyes at them and put my head back down. Ahmad leaned on my arm, and his hand went back to my stomach.

"Aye, Shyy was it Karra that said you could piss all over her R. Kelly style if you make her your girl?" Ahmad asked.

"Hell, yeah and a nigga just might," Shyy replied, and everybody including me laughed.

"Quiet down!" The sub yelled.

"Really, Ahmad? Y'all trying to play me out like that?" Karra asked with hurt in her tone. I chuckled at how stupid she sounded. She was no different than Portia. Thinking sex would get the guy, only for him to have sex with you and still leave. That's why I was still a virgin. So no one could have the pleasure of fucking me and then joking about it.

"Yeah, I am. You talking shit about Pia when she ain't never done nothing to you or Rowan. Y'all better fall the fuck back with that shit," he said right before the bell rang.

"Whatever, Ahmad," Karra retorted in a defeated tone. She knew once you made Ahmad's shit list it was over for you.

We all stood, and I made eye contact with Rowan once again. Her eyes narrowed into slits as she looked me up and down. She eventually smiled, then she walked off with her girls who were all hoes as well in tow. Ahmad grabbed my hand, and we walked out of class. He took me to an empty classroom, and we made out for an hour before it was time for him to prep for his game and for me to leave for Chicago to visit Portia.

"Oh hit that shit, Lay Lay! Aye!" Portia yelled and blew weed smoke out of her mouth. I watched Portia's friend drop down and make both of her ass cheeks bounce to the music. The room full of men and women clapped and threw money at her.

If I had known Portia was having a lingerie party tonight, I would have stayed my ass at home. Usually, I come with one of my brothers, but they didn't wanna come so I caught a flight alone.

I refused to put on the red lace teddy that Portia gave me. I had on my regular pajamas, and I was still uncomfortable with the way some of the men were gawking at me. I called Ahmad to see how his game went, but he didn't call me back. I guess he was busy partying too.

"Pia, dance on the pole, show them what you got from your Momma! My baby can dance her ass off y'all," she said and giggled. All of the men in the room gawked at me with greedy eyes. I quickly shook my head. I turned and damned near ran out of the room. Wasn't no way in hell I was dancing on that pole. I went to my bedroom and locked the door. I put my chair next to it. No one had ever raped me before, but

I had fought off two of Portia's boyfriends for attempting to molest me when I was younger. Ahmad was the only person besides my dad that knew about that. My dad handled them whatever that meant but still those near rape experiences had me shook.

Knock. Knock.

"Open the door Pia. It's only twelve and you going to bed? Get your boring ass out here," Portia said jiggling my door handle.

I noticed my soft pink bedroom hadn't been updated in years. Soon I would be seventeen, and I had just one more year that I had to see her after that I would be done with Portia.

"No, I'm cramping Portia. Leave me alone!" I yelled and grabbed my cell before going to my oversized chair. I sat down and saw that I had a text from an unknown number. I looked at it and smiled.

313-737-7644 *Zaria gave me your number. I'm at another school now so I never got to tell you this, but I'm feeling you Pia, this Xay (Xerius)*

I giggled. Damn, um okay.

Me: *Okay, thank you.*

Xerius: *Damn that's it? I see Ahmad got you trained already.*

I hated when people said that shit. I wasn't dating guys because I didn't want to date. Of course, I liked Ahmad, but he wasn't my master.

Me: *well I'm texting you so I must have some control over my life nigga.*

Xerius: *yeah that's what you say. Can I take you out?*

I got ready to reply when a text came in from Zaria.

Zaria: *Why is Ahmad and Rowan in the room at this party. I tried to take a picture of them, but Shyy threatened to break my fucking phone. Pia he fucking with that hoe again after all the shit she did to him.*

I sat my phone down and stared at the ceiling. This was the story of my life. Me fantasizing about life with Ahmad while he dated other chicks. I mean he was just sucking on my neck earlier while fingering me now he was with someone else? A couple or not he should not feel okay with doing shit like that. My phone buzzed again making me groan. I couldn't take too many more Ahmad text updates.

Xerius: *so me and you on a date or nah? What's up?*

I smiled, shit why not?

Me: *why not, next weekend I'm all yours.*

Xerius: *I know…lol*

I laughed getting ready to put my phone away when it started ringing. I looked at the ID and smiled. She was always thinking of me.

"Hey, Ma," I said taking the call.

"Hey, Pia. Is everything okay? You know I hate when you go out there with her," Sophie said sounding worried about me, and I could hear the girls in the background saying they missed me.

I sighed, as I laid back on one of my fluffy pillows.

"Yeah. I locked myself in the room," I replied.

"Listen, if you want to come home tomorrow just let me know. I will call Angel myself and argue with him about that," she said making me laugh because I knew she was serious. She didn't play.

"I know, and I appreciate you for that Ma. Guess what?"

She was quiet for a moment.

"Are you pregnant?" she asked quietly. I started laughing at her question.

"No! I'm still a virgin. I swear I am. I have a date, though. His name is Xerius, and he's cute. He looks like a dark-skinned version of the singer Chris Brown, but with chestnut colored eyes," I told her.

"Oh, he sounds cute. Now, how is my son gonna accept this news?" she asked.

I shrugged. Hell, who knows.

"Honestly, I don't know. I like him, but I'm not what he likes in a girlfriend, Ma and

I'm tired of watching him date while I'm just there waiting."

"Well, I think Ahmad is going to be happy with whatever you give him, but if you feel like my too-grown ass son is more advanced than you then yes don't rush it. You hold on to your virginity because it's something very precious. I wish Ahmad still had his. Don't conform to the ways of the world Pia. Be you and call me tomorrow. I always worry when you go out there. Love you, daughter," she said.

My heart warmed at her words. I couldn't imagine not having her in my life.

"I love you too, Ma," I said and ended the call. I put my phone down and smiled to myself. Ahmad was obviously fucking Rowan, so I didn't see how he could even find a way to be mad at me for going on a date with Xerius.

Chapter Four

Ahmad

My head was pounding, but I didn't let up as I played with my little cousin. His little ass was three going on ten. He was so damn grown. I guess I had something to do with that.

"Nah, give me the ball," he said and held his arms out.

I gently bounced it to him, and he bent down to get it. He laughed and tossed it as far as he could then laughed some more. It didn't take much to make his little ass happy. It took so much shit for me to put a smile on my spoiled ass sisters' faces. Shit. I'm not even gone get started on Pia. Damn. Just thinking about her had me feeling a little bit better.

"Ahmad! Ball!" He yelled and held out his arms again. I chuckled.

"Little nigga calm down," I said smiling.

"Yeah, his little ass ready," Mauri said walking onto the basketball court. Mauri was my older cousin and also an NBA player. I admired him so fucking much. I hoped he didn't take it personal when my time came, and I took all of his shine.

"Hell, yeah. He bad as hell," I said and tossed Aakil the ball again. My mom had surprised the shit out of us when she said she was pregnant, but I was relieved like a motherfucka when she said she was carrying a baby for my aunt, Erin. My aunt couldn't have any more kids so my moms did some shit that I don't think many women would have done. I was close with all of my cousins, but because my mom carried Aakil, I had a special connection with him. In my heart, he was more like my little brother than my cousin, and we always had his little ass along with his older brother KJ. I did laugh my ass off when I heard my moms tell my aunt that if she wanted a girl, my auntie Drew would have to pop her out, and my pops quickly co-signed that shit.

"So how school going?" Mauri asked. He was tall as hell, and I considered myself tall, yet he had me beat by some inches.

"It's going. Pia be on my ass, so I make sure I keep at least a 3.5 GPA," I replied as I watched Aakil.

"That what's up. You gotta have that book smarts too. So you ready to start visiting colleges and shit? I see your games on ESPN all the time. They ready for you," he said proudly. He'd been coaching me for years. I was in all kinds of ball camps when I was younger and had been given opportunities that I knew a lot of other ball players didn't have all because he played in the NBA. I owed him a lot. Shit, I had a lot of people investing in me to make it. I had no choice but to be great or get my ass kicked.

"Yeah, I hope Pia can come, though. I'm down to two choices, and I had her apply to both of them," I replied. Mauri looked at me with the same eyes that I had and he smirked. Our genes were strong as hell.

"Pia, Pia, Pia. I see she got yo ass where she wants you, but I feel it. Jess had a nigga the same way. I had it bad for her shit I still do," he said chuckling. "You gotta make sure you don't lose sight of what's important which is your career and your girl. Don't let these broads slip you up," he said and like clockwork Rowan walked onto the court with her flock of hoes following behind her. He looked back at them and slowly shook his head. He grabbed Aakil as Rowan walked over to us.

She was lucky my ma wasn't here, or her ass would have had to leave. My mom caught us fucking in the garage one time and after that, she banned Rowan from coming over. Man, I swear she fought me like a nigga on the streets while my pops stood back laughing. I was mad as hell.

"Hey, Ahmad and *Heyyy* Mauri. Can I get another autograph?" she asked and pulled a pen out of her purse. Mauri quickly signed her paper and looked at me.

"Remember what I said," he said before walking off with Aakil.

"Yep," I said and started dribbling the ball while Rowan stood in front of me. If I said she was just okay, I would be lying. Rowan was one of the finest bitches I had ever seen for her age. Her body was made for fucking, so sometimes hard to say no to it. I might fuck these bitches, but the only girl that would ever have my heart would be Pia, and if we were together, I wouldn't even be entertaining these hoes.

"So I was thinking about homecoming, and I figured we could go together," she suggested and bit down onto her plump bottom lip. I smiled as I shook my head.

"Come on, ma, be serious," I told her and stepped back so t I could bounce the ball between my legs. Rowan pouted, but that shit did nothing to me.

"Wow, so what I guess you taking Pia? The school teacher," she mocked making finger quotations. Yeah, Pia dressed super preppy but on her, it worked. I would rather she dress like that then a hoe.

"Cut it out before I embarrass you," I told her with a straight face. I hated when she started on Pia because it was nothing but hate. There's nothing worse than a jealous motherfucka.

Rowan's eyes watered, but she held her tears. She nodded and shifted from one foot to the other.

"You told me that you were single. When we were together you always talked about how much you were feeling me," she said taking a trip down memory lane.

For a minute, I had slipped up. Rowan started finally sucking my dick, and she was so good I agreed to shit I wouldn't usually do. She asked if we could be a couple, so I said yeah. Shit, my dick was all the way down her throat. Once Pia cut me off, I quickly came to my senses. Good head or not nothing was worth losing my girl.

"If that's true, then why are you always following after her. All up in her ass and shit. I mean it's all around the school how she fucking Xay," she said while frowning.

I stopped dribbling the ball and looked at her. Shit that was news to me. I hadn't heard no shit like that.

"You can go. I got shit to do," I told her and walked off. What pissed me off with Rowan was that if she couldn't get what she wanted from me, then she found a way to fuck up my day. I jumped in my pops' Bentley and called him up. He picked up on the third ring.

"Aye, Pops can I take the Bentley to Pia's house?"

He was quiet for a minute.

"Ahmad, if you scratch my car I'm fucking you up," he said and ended the call. I chuckled as I started up the sexiest car I had ever driven. I took my time and backed out of the garage then pulled off. I passed Rowan and saw her crying in her sports car while her friend rubbed her back. I felt bad, but damn she was putting herself through the pain. I never promised that girl shit. She can't even get free fucking water out of me, so why she felt like I would ever love her was lost on me.

Pia stayed ten blocks over from me. I wasn't sure how it happened I was just happy and hoping that her bitch ass pops didn't move anytime soon. My family still didn't fuck with that nigga and from what my uncles had said about him trying to get one over on my auntie I understood why. That was some bitch shit he did.

Once I made it to Pia's house, I texted her and told her I was outside. She came out a few minutes later in some leggings and a tank top. The way her hips moved in them had me hard. I didn't care what anyone said she was the most beautiful damn girl in the world to me. I loved everything about her long-necked ass.

She climbed into the car and looked around. My pops' Bentley was the shit. I pulled away as she put her seatbelt on.

"Hey, you," she said smiling. I was happy to see her, but I was more pissed at what Rowan had told me. I wasn't sure if the shit was true, but I was damn sure about to find out.

"So, the funniest shit happened today. I heard that you were fucking with that nigga Xerius," I said laughing only she didn't laugh with me. My hand gripped the steering wheel. "You wouldn't do no shit like that without talking to me, right? I mean you promised me at that fucking lake by my house that as my best friend you wouldn't do no hoe shit like that Pia," I reminded her.

Pia laughed and I damn near lost it. I drove to a nearby park and pulled into a deserted area. I turned to her and took off my seatbelt. She was wearing her glasses instead of her contacts, and she looked so sexy in her natural beauty.

"Ahmad, we were twelve. Like really. We're almost grown now," she said still smiling.

"Yeah, and you broke your promise when I never broke a promise to you. It's my blood running through you,"

I said thinking back on the blood oath we took. The shit was real to me. "When I see that nigga it's over for him and you." I pointed in her face to get my point across. "You gone stop entertaining that nigga. Cut that nigga the fuck off today Pia," I said glaring at her ass. Pia's nose flared as she looked back at me angrily. I didn't give a fuck if she was mad.

"What? No! You fucked all of them girls at our school Ahmad, and you are trying to tell me what to do? Xerius is nice, and he's okay with me being a virgin. He doesn't pressure me," she said like he was the perfect nigga for her. My body grew hotter at her words. Did I not teach her anything? These niggas will say and do whatever to get some pussy.

"That's what the fuck he saying now! Trust that nigga is gonna wanna hit it. I mean are you fucking dumb? You have to know that nigga is going to try something and just so you know he fucked Rowan too."

Pia smiled with sad eyes. I knew I was pushing it, but with her, I couldn't help it. I leaned towards her, and she looked away. I grabbed her face and gently kissed her on the lips. Even when she pissed me off, I still loved her ass.

"Stop fucking with him, Pia. I don't want him even near you," I whispered against her lips. Our eyes connected and she frowned. I kissed her again and slipped my hands between her legs. Easily, I put my hand into her leggings. I went into her underwear and down to my favorite new place. I was itching to taste her. Shit, to feel her but I knew with her

I had to be patient, and I didn't mind waiting. Shit, I had been waiting on Pia my whole damn life.

"This my shit Pia. Don't let him near it," I said inserting two fingers inside of her. Pia moaned, and her head fell back. I pulled down her cami and started sucking on her hard nipples. She started moaning loud and was getting wetter and wetter. My dick was on brick hard.

"Shit Pia… let's go get a room. No sex, but what we did last time," I told her.

"Ahmad…" I curved my fingers inside of her and bit her neck. "Okay, but no sex and we can't stay long," she quickly conceded. I smiled pulling my fingers out of her.

An hour later Pia and I were meeting my uncle, Kasam at a hotel near his recording studio. I could have called any of the men in my family, but on some real shit, Kasam was my fucking nigga. I love that nigga to death, and I knew he wouldn't lecture me and shit. He handed me the room key and a box of condoms. He told me not to make him a great uncle and left. That was why I fucked with him.

Pia sat on the bed shyly with no clothes on and a sheet wrapped around her sexy ass body. I know I said no sex, but damn I was hard as fuck, and she was just too beautiful. I wanted her first time to be more special than this, but shit this was a three-hundred dollar room. It wasn't a fucking motel.

"Pia, relax," I said sitting next to her. I moved the sheet away from her body and my mouth watered. Her breasts were perfect. I'd texted my dad and told him what my uncle did for me, and he told me I had two hours and not to drop Pia off pregnant. I guess they thought I was just out here fucking reckless. I had never had unprotected sex. Shit, I was scared of diseases, but Pia was different. She was clean, I guess they knew for her I had to hit it raw.

"You are so beautiful, damn," I said and kissed her. I started to kiss on her neck, and she fell back onto the bed. She still had her underwear on, and I was cool with that. I began to kiss my way down her body while she shivered at my touch.

For her comfort, the lights were off except for the bathroom but I could still see her beauty. She was made perfectly. No flaws and she was acting shy. Shit, she should have been proud to have this fucking body.

I grabbed her underwear and pushed them to the side. Pia had a fucking vice grip on my head with her thighs. I looked up at her, and she smiled nervously.

"Ma, ease up on your thighs. I know it's no sex. I just wanna taste you then I'mma show you how to do me. Okay?" I told her. She nodded, but I could see that the whole doing me part wasn't flying with her. Which was cool for now. I would show her how to effectively jack my shit off.

"Relax," I said and kissed her inner thigh. She instantly relaxed, and I ended up ripping her underwear. She sat up, and I started kissing on her juicy lower lips.

"Ahmad.... mmm.... damn," she moaned falling right back onto the bed. I opened them and slowly started to suck on her sweetness. I'd overheard one of my uncles saying no flavor was the best flavor and damn was he right. Pia tasted clean. She was the first and last person I knew I would ever go down on. I wasn't making no shit like this a habit.

"Ahmad…wait it feels funny," she said in this sexy ass voice. I smiled as I continued to suck on her clit. I listened to her body and let her moans show me how she likedher pussy licked. Quickly, I found my rhythm and her legs started to shake. I fingered her harder and sucked more vigorously on her. Soon she was cumming, and I was licking her juices away. I sat up and took off my Armani boxers. Pia looked at me with sated eyes while giving me a lazy grin. I could tell she was still feeling good.

"Ma, don't go to sleep. You gotta make sure I'm good too," I told her and pinched her cheek playfully. She nodded and sat up. I kissed her allowing her to taste herself on my tongue while I put her hand on my dick. I showed her how to stroke me like I had done before while I looked her in the eyes.

"You ain't gotta suck it, but just lick the tip. I need it, Pia. Can you do that for me?" I asked and kissed her again.

"I can," she replied quietly then slowly slid down my body. She took her time as she stared at my dick. I laid back and rested my hands behind my head. I waited and waited then waited some more. She quickly kissed the head before rushing back up towards me. Fuck, I wanted to yell I was so frustrated. Yes, Pia was a virgin, but this was me. She knew I would never do her like the niggas she saw dogging her moms out, but for some reason, she didn't believe that shit. She was allowing Portia's bullshit to keep us from connecting all the way.

I spat in my hand and started jacking myself off. I grabbed her hand and made her help me. Her chocolate-brown eyes slid over to mine, and she smiled sweetly. Sweet she was no doubt, but I wanted her to be nasty for me. The only time I saw her let loose was when she was in dance class. It was like she was another fucking person or something when she started popping that ass of hers all-around making my dick hard. I needed to find a way to pull that out of her in the bed.

"Kiss me," I told her. She licked her lips and leaned forward. I grabbed her face and stuck my tongue into her mouth. We kissed as her hand stroked my dick in a good rhythm. She squeezed the tip, and my balls tightened a little. I groaned and bit her bottom lip. "Make me cum. Make this dick squirt off," I said getting harder.

"Okay," she said and stroked me harder. It wasn't long before I was shooting off in her hand. She got up and washed her hand off, then my dick with a warm soapy wash rag. She got back in the bed with me and laid her head on my chest. I kissed the top of her head before yawning. I was tired than a motherfucka.

"Ahmad, we can't fall asleep," Pia said and yawned herself. I nodded with my eyes closed.

"I know just a nap, bae," I told her and drifted off to sleep with my hand on her ass.

My ringing cell phone jarred me awake hours later. I rubbed my eyes and slowly got up. I looked to my left and saw Pia was sound asleep beside me. I smiled as my finger slowly rubbed her hard ass nipple. She had some of the covers over the lower half of her body, and her mouth was hanging open with some drool on the side of her face. She was knocked the fuck out. Still, she looked beautiful. I guess love made you like everything about a person even the shit you would usually turn your nose up at.

My phone started ringing again, and I groaned. I grabbed it off of the nightstand and looked at the screen. My eyes shifted to the clock, and I jumped out of bed.

"Ma! Let me explain..."

"Explain what? How I have to lie to Pia's father because you and her done decided to spend the fucking night together? Huh! You are not fucking grown Ahmad! You are sixteen years old. Get your black ass to the house right fucking now and bring her with you so I can take her ass home," she said and ended the call.

I sighed looking over all of the text messages I had received over the night. The scariest ones were definitely from my uncles and my pops.

Kasam: *Damn I help you out, and you do me like this? I can't save you against your moms. She's fucking nuts nigga she tried to whoop* *me. I told your auntie if she does that shit again to beat her ass sister or not.*

Pops: *You gone pull some shit like this? Kasam said you won't answer the room door. Get your ass home. Angel is losing his mind. I don't wanna have to hurt this nigga. Come home!!*

I chose not to look at the other messages especially the ones from my moms and aunties. I could only imagine what the fuck they were saying to a nigga. I got back in bed and gently pushed Pia's arm until she slowly woke up. She rubbed her eyes for a moment before looking my way.

"Ahmad, what time is it?" she asked stretching out on the bed. I bit down hard on my bottom lip as I stared at her body. Damn, I wanted her so bad.

"It's seven o'clock," I replied and licked my lips. She smiled, making her breasts bounce.

"Oh okay, well I'mma wash up, and we can go," she said looking well rested. I grabbed her soft hand and showed her my phone's time. Pia's eyes damn near popped out of her head.

"Ahmad! Oh, my god! It's seven o'clock in the fucking morning! What the fuck!" she yelled.

Pia snatched her hand away from mine and ran around the room looking for her clothes while I stared at her body. I slowly got off of the bed and walked up behind her as she grabbed her leggings off of the floor. I wrapped my arms around her waist and poked my erection into her ass. Shit, we were already in trouble. There was no need to rush.

"Ma…you feel that," I said and slid my hands in between her legs. Pia stopped moving, and I slowly rubbed my fingers through her silky folds. She was wet as hell.

"Ahmad…no," she protested but didn't move my fingers. My phone started ringing again fucking the mood all up. Man, what the hell! Damn, they were just gone blow my shit up.

I let Pia go and grabbed my phone while she put her clothes on. I looked at the screen and shook my head. They were starting to piss me off. I silenced my mom's call and quickly got dressed. Pia and I rushed out of the room and headed back to my house in silence. She was so scared she started to bit down on her nail. I wasn't sure if she knew it, but she always did that when she felt like she was about to be in trouble.

When we were thirteen, she had snuck some of her pops beer into the garage for us, and we drunk one together. She was scared for a whole fucking week that he would find out. She had chewed all of her damn nails off worrying about it.

I leaned over as I stopped at a red light and kissed her on the cheek.

"We good, ma just relax. I'll take the blame for everything, and I know my ma got you covered," I reassured her. Pia glanced over at me with worried eyes and she nodded.

"I left my damn glasses, and he's gonna put me on punishment or maybe worse Ahmad," she replied. My face frowned up as I pulled away. Fuck she means by that?

"What's worse?" I asked not giving a fuck about her glasses shit I could get her some more.

"I don't know. Lately, he's been saying that he is thinking of moving back to Mexico. I heard him tell Primo that yesterday. I'm not sure if he means it, but I know that's what he said," she replied. I cleared my throat as I turned onto my block.

"Pia, I would never let him take you away from me. I can promise you that, ma," I said, and I could see her visibly relax. Shit, I would do whatever the fuck I had to do to keep her with me.

As I pulled up to my house, I spotted all three of my uncles' cars out front of the garage. I groaned and pulled my pops' Bentley into the last garage door. I closed the garage, and the lights cut on. I looked over at my baby and licked my lips.

"Look, they not gone say shit to you, and truthfully I don't regret shit. I just hate you have to get into it with your pops behind this shit. One last kiss before we are on lock down?" I asked and leaned towards her. Pia looked at me and immediately shook her head no. I chuckled, thinking she was playing, and the driver's door was snatched open. Something hit my arm hard as hell making me wince.

"Ah, what the fuck!" I yelled and was hit again. My damn moms was hitting me with a fucking thick ass belt! I tried to get out of the car, and she hit my arm hard as hell.

"Ah damn! Okay, I'm sorry!" I yelled, shielding my face. I could hear my pops and uncles laughing hard as hell.

"Nah, it's no okay, you staying out all night like you fucking grown when you not!" she yelled and started whipping my legs. That shit hurt bad as fuck!

"Ah! Shit! Damn! Okay, Ma! Aye, Pops really!" I yelled with my legs on fire.

"Aye, Sophie, okay man damn," my pops said grabbing her by the waist and chuckling. He pulled her away, and I sighed with relief. I leaned my head against the steering wheel trying to slow down my rapidly beating heart while my uncles clowned me.

"Man, that shit was too fucking funny!" Kasam said and laughed harder. I slowly got out of the car and my damn left leg wobbled almost making me fall. She had fucked that one up the worst. I leaned on the car for support as I slowly closed the car door.

"Damn she done disabled this little nigga," Aamil, my oldest uncle said laughing at me.

"Hell, yeah, I should have brought his ass a cane or some shit," My other uncle, Kadar cut in. These niggas were going in on me.

"Y'all niggas really funny," I told them still pissed off.

My mom walked back into the garage and I looked at her. She seemed like a fucking deranged woman with her hair all over her head and shit. She started walking towards me, and I hopped around the Bentley with my good leg to the other side which made my uncles laugh harder.

"Hell, nah this shit too funny, this nigga bouncing like old girl off *I'm Gonna Git You Sucka.* I gotta record this shit!" Kasam yelled pulling out his cell phone.

"Ma! Wait! I'm sorry. I swear we fell asleep and didn't realize it," I told her. She stopped walking and glared my way. I noticed Pia was also on the side of the car with my Auntie Erin standing next to her. I had always been my auntie's favorite. I hopped over to Erin and looked at her with pleading eyes. She glared at me for a moment before slowly softening her face. She turned to my mom, her oldest sister and sighed.

"Sophie, let him be, sis. Please take Pia home before Angel comes back over here," she said with her eyes glancing my Auntie Olivia's way. I wasn't sure what that shit was about.

"Hell yeah, that nigga talking too reckless. Looking at "O" like he in love and shit," my Uncle Kadar said no longer laughing.

"Ahmad, drop that phone off to your father now, and we'll talk when I get back. Let's go Pia and you both should know that I am very disappointed with you," she said before walking away. I exhaled and hugged my aunt. Shit, I was scared she was going to try to whoop me again.

"Do better Ahmad," Erin said patting my back.

"I promise I will Auntie," I said looking down at her. I was at the point where I was towering over all of my aunts even my mom.

"I will Auntie, I promise," I said meaning it. I had no intention of staying out all night.

I tried to hug Pia, and my aunt cock blocked me, so I tapped her thigh and hopped off while she left with my Ma. I went inside and hopped to my pops' office. He sat in the room smoking on a blunt while ESPN played on his flat screen on the wall. I closed the door and sat on the sofa furthest away from him. I wasn't ashamed to admit this nigga scared the life out of me. I respected him a lot. At one point in time, he and my uncles were Detroit drug kingpins. My Pops said it took a lot of blood, sweat and tears, but they were able to go legit. I respected him for that. He never showed me any of that shit when I was younger, so I thought he had a regular fucking job and shit.

"You wanna be a dad," he asked me blowing smoke out of his mouth. I looked at him. His eyes were the same shade of hazel as mine. He was tall with lighter skin than mine and he had a bald head. He also had a long ass beard that he kept groomed like all of my uncles. I was trying to grow my beard on their level and shit.

"Nah, Pops you know I don't."

He hit his blunt a few more times and cleared his throat.

"Ahmad, you gotta do better. Yeah, you fucking up the basketball court but you slacking with Pia. Y'all spending a lot of time together and if this persists she might end up pregnant. Your moms is too fucking fine to be a grandma so soon. Plus, that shit would gut her. I hustled hard for you to be able to live a carefree good life. Chill out, and just enjoy being a teenager," he told me. I understood what he was saying because that's what I had been doing. Parents always felt like because you were under eighteen you ain't know shit. I chose to say what he wanted to hear versus how I felt.

"Pops, I'mma do better. That was my fault, and it won't happen again."

He looked me in the eyes and chuckled.

"Ahmad, don't feed me no bullshit. Get your shit together before Angel take Pia away from you. You know he is looking for a reason to keep her away any fucking way. Why are you helping? You must not want her around," he said and went back to smoking his blunt. I slowly stood and looked down at him.

"Pops, I'mma be okay and so will Pia," I said before hopping away. Fuck what he and everybody else was saying. Angel wasn't doing shit if I had a say so in it.

Chapter Five

Pia

"You know I'm not the bad guy. I didn't decide to spend the night at the Matins' house," my dad said smiling at me. I looked away and sighed. This was my worst nightmare confirmed.

"This is for the best and Michigan is getting to be *old* to me anyways. I'll let you finish this school year, and we will move next summer," he said before standing up and walking out my room.

I watched his back exit through my bedroom door, and my tears escaped my eyes. For him this was for the best however for me, it wasn't. I didn't want to fucking go back to Mexico. My life was here in Michigan with Ahmad.

He said he wasn't punishing me for being with Ahmad, but I knew that he was. He already hated that I still talked with Ahmad and his family, but for him to know I stayed the night with Ahmad was too much for him to handle. I got out of my bed and left my room. I went to my father's bedroom and slowly stepped in. He sat in his black leather chair with his eyes on the basketball game. My dad was so handsome. I don't know what the hell Portia was thinking when she left him. He was genuinely a good man, and I loved him with all of my heart.

"Dad, can we please just talk about this? I don't wanna leave the country," I pleaded sitting by his leg. He ignored me, I continued to speak as I leaned against him. "I'm still a virgin, I swear. Like Sophie said they went out, and Ahmad and I fell asleep in the basement. When they came in, they didn't know I was there, and we didn't do anything. I promise you I didn't have sex with him," I said adamantly.

"Pia, the Matins are not good people. They're into all kinds of illegal shit, baby. I don't trust them, and it's only because of my love for you that I allow you to even go over there. I don't trust Ahmad. You need to focus on school and leave him alone for a while. If you can promise to spend more time at home and with your female friends, then maybe we can stay. If you stay on this path that you're on with him, I will be forced to take you away. I refuse to lose you to him," he said. I sighed hugging his leg. I would always be his daughter so how was he losing me to Ahmad? More so how could I stay away from the one person I loved with all of my heart?

"Dad, I'll do it," I said rolling my eyes. I would agree to just about any damn thing as long as it resulted in me staying in Michigan.

"Pia, I mean it. Let Ahmad focus on basketball and school and you concentrate on your studies and dance. No more studying with him or even going to his house and no more babysitting for any of them. You need to worry about yourself. Fuck them shady ass motherfuckas," he said vehemently, and I held in my cries as my eyes watered. He was going to pull this card on me like I was five years old. This was crazy. *****

"What the fuck do you mean you can't come home with me?" Ahmad asked as we exited the school. I looked at him and shook my head. I glanced around the parking lot, and my eyes landed on my two-door black Mercedes. I never drove my car because I always rode with Ahmad, but my dad forced me to drive because I was on my *no* Ahmad and *no* Matin family punishment.

"Ahmad, I can't. Part of my punishment is me staying away from you."

Ahmad's hazel eyes darkened. He grabbed my arm and pulled me towards him.

"What the fuck are you talking about Pia?"

I looked up at him and sighed. All he got was that whooping from Sophie then he was good. He had to have known I was going to get in trouble as well. What did he think my dad was going to say about me staying the night with him?

"My dad said that if I don't stay away from you, he's going to take me to Mexico, Ahmad."

Ahmad's eyes widened, as he took a step back pulling me with him. He dropped his head, and a light chuckle left his mouth.

"Pia, you and I both know that's not happening," he said like he really had a say so over if I left or not.

"Ahmad, we just need to give it a month maybe, and he'll be cool," I suggested glancing at him.

"Nah, fuck that. Call up Zaria and have her cover for you. I need for you to roll with me real quick," he said leading us over to his car. He opened the door, and I stopped him from pushing me into the seat.

"Ahmad, this is serious! If I get caught hanging out with you that could be it for us," I told him getting upset with his careless attitude. This shit wasn't a game.

Ahmad put his hoodie on his head and looked at me. His eyes were a mixture of pain, anger, and sadness. He placed his hands on top of his old school car and licked his lips.

"Today is my real mom's birthday. You gone say fuck a nigga today? I need you "P"," he said sounding so vulnerable it pulled at my heart strings.

"I'll follow you," I told him and walked off. I called Zaria as I got into my car.

"Hey trick, I was looking for you," she said answering the call.

"Hey, I need for you to tell your mom me and you are going to the mall to look for jobs just in case my dad checks up on me. I'mma ride out with Ahmad really quick," I told her as I followed him out of the lot.

Zaria sighed on the other end of the phone.

"Okay, I can do that, but what about us going to get our nails done? I mean you and Ahmad can't take one fucking day away from each other," she said angrily. I frowned not liking the way she was coming at me.

"Zaria, we're friends, but we're not in a relationship so don't act like I gotta spend all of my time with you."

Zaria laughed.

"Well, you're not in a relationship with Ahmad either, so I would watch how much time I gave to someone that was giving his time to everybody," she said before ending the call.

"Bitch," I mumbled as I put my phone away. I was gonna cool it on her ass. She was slowly starting to get on my fucking nerves.

Silently, I followed Ahmad to his mother's gravesite after he stopped to get her flowers. I shot his mom a text to let her know what was going on after parking. We walked to the grave hand in hand, he replaced her old flowers with the new ones. We sat down and leaned against it. Ahmad decided to stretch out and lay his head in my lap with his eyes closed. Talking about his biolgical mother, Tatum was always a touchy subject. He only knew that she was killed and found wrapped naked in a blanket. He said it didn't bother him, but I wasn't so sure. I knew that a part of him still missed and loved her no matter how much love he had for Sophie, his stepmother.

"A part of me wonders what it would be like if she was alive. If she would be proud of me and the shit I'm doing or if she would be like she was in the past. Just all about herself and shit. My memories of her are so vague maybe she did love me, and I just forgot. I mean I was young as fuck," he said while I rubbed my hand over the waves in his jet black hair.

"How could she not love you, Ahmad? You were her son. I'm sure she loved you very much," I told him believing what I had said.

He kissed my hand and briefly I closed my eyes to enjoy the feel of his lips against my skin. It felt like it had been forever since he kissed me.

"Then why did she leave me? Why is she not here right now, Pia?" he asked in a throaty tone then cleared his voice.

"She was dealing with her own issues, but she loved you," Ameer said startling Ahmad and me. I hadn't even noticed him and Sophie walking up. I was happy to see that they had come. Ahmad looked at him, and I noticed Ahmad had red swollen eyes. He slowly stood and hugged his dad before he hugged Sophie. Sophie whispered something to him, and he nodded before burying his face into her shirt. She pulled him away from the grave, and Ameer sat down next to me while she and Ahmad shared their moment.

"I appreciate you for texting Sophie. You're a good girl, Pia," he said with a head nod. I hoped he knew I would do anything for his son. When he was in pain, it was like I was experiencing it as well.

"I was just worried about him. He has so many unanswered questions, you know. He sometimes talks about finding his family on her side and reconnecting with them," I said making Ameer give me this funny look. He quickly shook his head like that was a crazy idea or something.

"Nah, he doesn't need to do that. If they gave a fuck about him, then they would have been in the picture. Fuck them," he said with a little anger in his tone.

I looked straight ahead not sure if I agreed with him on that as Ahmad and Sophie walked back over to us. They sat down, and I hugged Sophie briefly.

"What was her favorite movie, Pops?" Ahmad asked.

Ameer looked at him and smiled.

"New Jack City. She loved all of that gangster shit. I remember she used to watch Scarface back to back. She also liked black and white movies because your grandfather watched them with her when she was younger, but he's dead now too. He died when she was sixteen," Ameer replied.

"So how did you meet her?"

Ameer rubbed his hand over his bald head.

"I was at the mall, and I saw this fly ass girl going into the music store. I tried to talk to her, but she shot me down. Later on that week, I saw her in the city, and we started talking. From there it was on. She was so full of life. She loved to be in the mix of some shit. Even after she had you we were still traveling and enjoying life and shit."

Ahmad smiled and laid his head back onto my lap.

"Then why did you divorce her? What happened? Who killed her?"

Ameer looked at Sophie and Sophie shook her head. I could tell this was making them a little uncomfortable.

"We grew apart Ahmad. It's fucked up that it happened, but it did and then I met Sophie. Your mom started kicking it with somebody she knew from down south, and it was all bad from there," Ameer replied.

"But she left me. Why? Didn't she love me? Did you make her leave me?" he asked still full of questions. I rubbed his waves to calm him down; I could tell he was getting himself worked up.

"Ahmad, I love you, so yeah if she would have tried to take you I would have put up a fight, but she didn't. She did love you, though, son," he responded.

Ahmad shook his head.

"I'm just confused on so much shit pops. Why can't I talk to my grandmother on her side?" he asked.

Ameer's light face started to turn red.

"Because they don't give a fuck about you, Ahmad! Like what the fuck don't you get? I told you how they are. A bunch of selfish motherfuckas. They gone be on you now that they know you are playing ball. Where the fuck were they when you needed them? Fuck them!" Ameer yelled, and Sophie whispered something in his ear as Ahmad sat up.

"I got a right to fucking meet them," he said angrily. I grabbed his arm and gave it a light squeeze.

Ameer jumped up, and Ahmad did too snatching his arm away from me. Ameer walked up on Ahmad and glared down at him. Tall or not Ahmad was still shorter than his dad.

"Say that shit again," he told him, and Sophie and I both stood up. I grabbed Ahmad's hand and tried to pull him back some. It was like pulling a truck because his ass wouldn't step back.

Ahmad and Ameer stared each other down until Ahmad looked away. He looked back at Ameer with a calmer face.

"All I wanna do is know about the woman that brought me into this world. You wrong as fuck for stopping me from doing that," he said, and Ameer grabbed him by his throat.

"Ameer! Calm down," Sophie said grabbing his arm.

Ameer held a tight grip on Ahmad as he looked in his eyes. He had him by the throat, but it was evident he wasn't applying real pressure.

"Ahmad, I love you more than I love my fucking self, so if I stop you from doing anything, it's for your own good. You belong to me, and I refuse to let a motherfucka play you regardless of who the fuck they are. You are my fucking son!" he yelled and pulled him into a hug. Ahmad broke down again as he hugged him and Sophie and I stood by and watched the father and son mourn the loss of Ahmad's mother.

Chapter Six

Ahmad

Me: *Hey you missed my fucking game. I'm pissed.*
Me: *Can you at least call me back?*
Me: *Are you coming with me to the homecoming dance?*

"Really, Ahmad? You gone ignore me the whole time?"

I put my phone down and saw Rowan standing in front of me in her birthday suit looking good as fuck. Feeling defeated I took a hit from my blunt. I wasn't much of a smoker but these last few weeks without my girl by my side had me stressed, then I had all of these unanswered questions about my mom, and my fucking pops refused to help me with them. I would even ask my uncles, and they would say some shit like "we don't wanna get into that shit." They were all on some hush, hush shit for some reason.

"I'm good. I just got a lot on my mind," I replied, blowing smoke out of my mouth. Rowan smiled as she dropped down to her knees. She started stroking my dick, and I wished that it could be Pia between my legs pleasing me. I was trying to be understanding with her, but I was starting to get pissed the fuck off.

"Well let me help you out," Rowan said, still stroking me. I groaned as her warm mouth covered the tip. My phone vibrated, and I quickly grabbed it.

Pia: *of course I'm still going with you and my dad is going to Miami that weekend so I can stay with you if you want*

I smiled hard as hell at that text. Homecoming was two weeks away, and I couldn't wait.

Me: *hell yeah I want you to. I miss you. A lot.*

Pia: *I miss you too. I'm with Portia, and so I will call you later. Sorry, I missed your game. I know you did good because I called ma. Ahmad I*

"Shit," I said dropping the phone. Rowan was sucking the skin off of my dick. I grabbed the phone off of the ground. I looked at Pia's text, and my dick grew even harder.

Pia: *I miss you too. I'm with Portia, and so I will call you later. Sorry, I missed your game. I know you did good because I called ma. Ahmad, I want you to make love to me. Can you? I don't wanna wait any longer.*

Me: *yeah I can do that ma.*

Pia: *Ok*

I put my phone on the dresser and grabbed Rowan's head. I closed my eyes and imagined she was Pia topping me off. I bit down hard on my bottom lip and guided her up and down onto my shit. Damn. Two weeks couldn't get here fast enough!

"Ahmad! Stop!" Rowan yelled fucking up the moment. I let go of her head, and she jumped up. She wiped her mouth while angrily looking at me.

"What?" I asked with my dick still hard and covered in her saliva.

"You fucking called me Pia, nigga that's what. Take me home!" she yelled getting all hype and shit.

"Alright, I got you just pipe your ass down," I said putting my shit away, and she smacked her lips.

"Oh, so, no, baby I'm sorry? Nigga, you are so fucking fake. I swear," she said and stomped off cursing and shit. I could give less than two fucks about her attitude. I got up and washed myself off before I put back on my clothes. I walked out of the hotel bedroom with an angry Rowan. A few people from my basketball team were still partying, but mostly everybody had dipped off and got a room.

Rowan walked to the door as my eyes connected with Zaria's. This bitch had her phone in her hand, and it was pointed directly at me. I stopped mid-step and walked over to that hoe. This little nappy headed bitch was going to make me fuck her ass up, and I had never put my hands on a female.

"Bitch, give me that shit,'" I said, trying to grab her phone. This bitch put that shit in her bra and smirked at me. It wasn't that Zaria was even ugly, she was just a hoe. I mean she had been letting niggas fuck her since middle school, and she was always trying to tell Pia about the shit I was doing. She failed to mention how she begged to suck my dick for years until finally, I threatened to tell Pia, and she let up. That was the real reason she was mad at a nigga. She wished she was my baby.

"Nah, she needs to see with her own eyes how much of a hoe you are," she said with a sly ass smirk on her face. I chuckled as I stroked my small beard. This bitch wanted to play games.

"Look, I'm not about to argue with your big headed, teeth so fucking yellow it looks like you got a fucking gold grill ass. If you send Pia that video or photo I'mma slap the shit out of you." Zaria smiled and rolled her eyes. This bitch thought I was playing. I'm not a nice nigga. I'm nice to Pia because I love her, these other hoes will never see that side of me.

"Aye, April come here!" I yelled. April was one of the female basketball players. I fucked with her from time to time because she had ass for days, but she always knew to keep it on the low, and that was why I liked her.

"Hey what's up, Ahmad?" she asked looking from me to Zaria. Zaria was still smirking, but that shit was about to change really quickly.

"Hey, I got five hundred dollars if you beat this bitch ass for me," I said and pulled some money out of my jogging pants that my uncle Kasam had just given me for winning the game. I handed April five one hundred dollar bills, and she smiled like she had hit the lottery.

April put the money in her pants pocket, and her hand swung back and slapped the spit out of Zaria's mouth.

"Oh, shit! April, get that bitch!" Shyy yelled running over with his phone. I slapped theat shit out of his hand and shook my head at him. This nigga was trying to get us expelled or worse.

"Bitch!" Zaria yelled and ran to April, who was in a boxer's stance.

Whap! Whop!

"Damnnnn!" We all yelled.

April two-pieced the fuck out of Zaria and Zaria fell back making her phone fall out of her cleavage. I dropped down and picked it up as April began to drag Zaria out of the hotel room kicking and screaming. We were all laughing at her stupid ass, and the bitches she had come with wasn't even trying to help her. Scary ass hoes.

I looked through Zaria's phone and erased the pics that she had taken of me with Rowan. Her nosey ass had even taken a few pictures of us at the game together and shit. This bitch was too lonely because any hoe with a life would not have time to do all of this. I sat her phone down on a nearby table, and Rowan walked up on me with angry eyes.

"I don't like Zaria, but that was wrong. What did she do to you?" she asked with a worried look in her eyes. I hoped she knew she would get that same treatment if she ever tried to do some harm to Pia.

"Nothing that concerns you, now let's go before I have April handle your ass, too," I said only half-joking. We walked out of the room, and I watched Zaria's girls pull her down the hallway as she tried to adjust her torn clothes and fucked up hair. I threw her the deuces as we walked past them.

"Take it easy, bitch," I said chuckling.

"My brother is going to fuck you up! Stupid nigga" she yelled at me. Her brother was a supposed crip. Like nigga how you in a gang and you have a fucking maid in your house? That nigga was a lame. See no matter who my family was I never pretended to be something I wasn't. I was a crazy nigga, but I never claimed to be hood because truthfully I knew nothing about that.

"Tell that nigga to run up if he wants to and I'mma do him worse than April did you," I yelled over my shoulder.

After dropping Rowan off at her sister's crib, me and Shyy went to kick it with my uncles at the studio. The minute we stepped in a billow of weed smoke greeted us. I smiled fanning that shit out of my face. If I went home smelling like weed, my moms was going to fuck me up again.

"Look at this nigga! My little MJ and shit! Winning his uncle, them bands!" Kasam yelled jumping up from his seat. I hugged him then I hugged Kadar and Aamil. I sat down, and Shyy sat next to me. I stretched out and looked at my uncles. Fuck a celebrity or public figure these niggas were who the fuck I looked up to.

They all owned their own shit and was living the life. I respected the way they held down their families and shit. They were real fucking men and I felt honored to have them in my life to show me what a real man was because so many black men didn't have that. These niggas wouldn't let me fail, and you need people like that in your life to push you.

"So what's up? How was the party?' Aamil asked and blowing some weed smoke out of his mouth. I shrugged, but that nigga Shyy laughed. This nigga couldn't hold fucking water, but he was my nigga and had been my friend since we were young ass kids.

"Man, this nigga Ahmad had this fine-ass, big, booty basketball bitch beat up Pia's friend. That shit was funny as hell," he said chuckling.

My uncles laughed, and Aamil passed me his blunt. I took it and did a few hits before passing it to Shyy.

"Man, it wasn't even like that. This bitch was taking pictures of me with Rowan and shit. I couldn't let her send that to Pia. She would have come home mad at me over some dumb shit when she knows I don't give a fuck about Rowan," I replied.

"Hmm, but you fucking her though so she probably thinks you do. You not raw dogging that bitch is you?" Kasam asked looking at me. I quickly shook my head.

"Hell, nah! And bring a baby up in my fucking house? My moms would murk me. The only person she would even accept a kid from is Pia," I said, and they all nodded knowing

I was telling the truth. "But, we not even on that shit. We got plans and kids can wait. I just want Pia with me when I make it. Her hoe ass pops talking about taking her to Mexico unless she stays away from me and shit. I hate that nigga," I said shaking my head.

"Man, that nigga. He still salty Omari isn't his. Following "O" on all her social media accounts and shit on some stalker type shit. Fuck Angel, fuck his momma for not being on birth control. Fuck his pops for not wrapping it up. Shit fuck the nigga that delivered him," Kadar said making us all laugh. Kasam looked at him.

"Nigga you's a fool," he said and laughed again. Pia's pops Angel had crept with my aunt Olivia who was Kadar's wife before they got married and she thought that he was Omari, my little cousin's father. It turned out that he wasn't, and Angel was mad about it. What was fucked up was that he was doing business with my family at the time that he was kicking it with Olivia. He was just a shady ass nigga.

"But that nigga might do it to hurt me. I can't let that shit happen," I said placing my elbows on my knees.

"How the fuck you gone stop him though Ahmad?" Aamil asked and drunk something out of a red cup.

I sighed. Shit, that was the million dollar question. How the fuck was, I going to stop this nigga? This crazy ass idea popped into my head making me laugh.

"Shit, I might have to trap her ass, bitches do it all of the time to keep a nigga," I said and them niggas laughed, but

I was serious as hell. Kasam noticed I wasn't laughing and quickly shook his head.

"Ahmad, no. Look, I like Pia and yeah she is down for you but you young as fuck. Who knows who you gonna end up with. You turning seventeen tomorrow. You have your whole fucking life ahead of you. You don't need no fucking baby," he said, and they all nodded agreeing with him. Shit, I didn't even want a baby, but to keep *my* baby, I would damn sure give her a baby.

Chapter Seven

Pia

"So where are we gonna live?"

I smiled and looked over at him. His eyes were closed, and he was grinning real hard. Like a damn kid on Christmas morning. I had missed his big headed self so much. The minute I touched down in Michigan, I went straight to him. I told my dad I had something to do with Zaria. I tried to call her, but she didn't answer. Oh well, at this point I didn't even care. If I got caught, I would cross that road when I got to it. Seeing Ahmad at school wasn't enough for me. We only had one class together.

I was used to spending every day with him. Even when he worked out and went to practice, I usually tagged along. The only time I wouldn't see him was when I was in dance class. I used to do ballet but gave that up when I moved to Michigan. Now I did hip-hop dancing, and I loved it. I also did gymnastics, but eventually stopped going to that one, too. Hopefully, I could have my own non-profit dance studio for low-income mothers someday. Dancing had always been such a happy place for me, and I wanted to give that to little girls that wouldn't normally have an opportunity to dance because dance school was expensive as hell.

"I wanna live in a house kind of like yours, Ahmad. I don't want any neighbors, and if we do have some, they better be far as hell away from us. I like how your house is enclosed on its own land. I want a lake too and a big bathroom and closet. I mean the bathroom has to have a huge bathtub with his and her sinks and everything," I replied imagining how our future home would look.

Ahmad grabbed my hand. It was a little cold outside, but we had our blankets, and we were chilling. This was our spot by the lake where we always shared our hopes and dreams.

"What about kids?" He asked quietly. I glanced over at him and smiled. We had never discussed children before.

"I don't know. Between your sisters and cousins, we won't need any. Soraya would kill me if I had a baby," I said and laughed. Soraya was like my mini-me. She always wanted all of my attention.

Ahmad rolled over and climbed on top of me. He covered us with the blanket, and he kissed my lips. I opened my eyes and peeked at him.

"What?" I asked smiling. He was staring at me with such an intense expression on his handsome face. He shook his head and kissed me again. I'd just given him his birthday gift which was a watch with our initials engraved on it and he was wearing it. Ever since I got with him, he had been acting weird, though.

"What if I said I wanna be with you like on some real you my woman and I'm your man type shit?" he asked. I shrugged with butterflies brewing in the pit of my stomach. Was he serious?

"Is this because I said I wanted us to have sex? I mean I want you to wanna be with me not feel obligated to do it."

"Nah, it's not that. I'm just trying to see where yo head at. I'm tired of playing games with these hoes out here. I wanna be with you and only you Pia. No Rowan or anyone else just you like it's always been. All that talk of you possibly leaving got me scared. I see now that you're not automatic. We could die tonight, and I have to leave this earth knowing what it's like to be your man. So what do you say?" he asked again. My eyes watered, and a tear slipped from my eye. I couldn't believe this was happening.

"I say hell fucking yeah," I said, and we both laughed before he kissed me so hard it took my breath away.

"Aye, Zaria come here!" I yelled running behind her. I was so fucking mad I didn't know what to do. I grabbed her arm, and she snatched it back and turned around scowling at me. I frowned at her attitude. How the hell was she mad at me? I was the one in trouble because of her.

"Why did you tell my dad I was with Ahmad yesterday. I'm on fucking punishment again because of you," I said in a low voice trying to keep the conversation between us.

Zaria laughed, and it was then that I noticed one of her teeth was missing on the left side of her mouth. She was also sporting a black eye.

"Fuck you and that nigga!" She yelled pushing me so hard I fell. Before I could get up, she was climbing on top of me and punching me in my face while somebody was kicking me in my side.

"Bitch, all I have ever been was a good friend to you! You so fucking stupid and you ain't all that! With your mutt ass!" She yelled and punched me in my mouth. I was able to hit her back before someone else jumped in and started kicking my legs.

"Damn! Aye, go get Ahmad!" I could faintly hear someone yell. I blocked her hits as best as I could until someone kicked me in my head so hard that my vision blurred.

I awoke in a well-lit room. I tried to sit up but couldn't. My body was beyond sore. I groaned, and someone grabbed my hand.

"Relax, Princess," my dad said through clenched teeth. I sighed because I knew this wasn't good.

"Dad, where am I?' I asked still covering my eyes with my arm because my head was pounding.

"You're in the hospital. You have a concussion because you were jumped by some girls because of Ahmad," he said coldly.

My heart beat sped up at his words. How did he know this was because of Ahmad? Zaria had been acting funny for a while now.

"Dad, my head," I said and whined. I was sore all over.

"Let me go get the nurse," he said letting my hand go.

"So, when will you believe me when I say those Matin men are fucking trash, shit the women are too," Portia said from the other side of me. Why the fuck was she even here?

"Look fuck all of that. Who did this to you? Somebody said it was Zaria," Primo said angrily.

"It was Primo," I said and slightly shook my head. Hell, I was ashamed to admit it was her. I mean why would she do this?

"Oh, I got that bitch," he said.

"Ahmad fucked her. That's what men do, baby. They fuck your friends if they can," she said and giggled. What the hell was funny about this?

"Portia enough," my dad said, stepping back into the room. A nurse began to talk to me and soon my I.V. was being filled with liquid medicine that had me higher than a kite. I relaxed and fell asleep as my dad told me I would never see Ahmad again.

Chapter Eight

Pia

Homecoming and a few holidays came and went. Soon it was a new year and for the first time in five years, I didn't get to tell my best friend, the love of my life happy new year. My heart was broken something terrible. I held my book bag tightly to my chest as I walked down the hall of my new school, that just so happened to be the private school Xerius attended. I hadn't talked to him since Ahmad begged me not to. I was so distraught over not being with Ahmad that I didn't know what to do. I was a shell of a fucking person. Here it was my birthday, and I was in school with no new outfit on or a new hairdo. I was just here, existing but not living. I had no cell phone, and my dad had my brothers drive me to and from school. I had called Sophie a couple of times, but she said that things with them and my dad were strained and for me to stay back until she could get it worked out. I loved and trusted her, so I was taking her word on it but still I wanted to see *him*. Hug him, hell just be up under him.

"Hey, sit with me at lunch Sweet P," Xerius said walking up to me. I nodded and kept walking. He looked me over, and a crooked smile slid across his face.

"I mean you and that nigga must have really been in love. You walking around like a zombie and shit then I heard from one of my boys that he stopped playing ball. Y'all is really going through it," he said sounding sad for me. I ceased to walking at his words. Wait what?

"What do you mean he stopped playing?"

Xerius licked his lips as he looked down at me.

"He stopped playing basketball. He quit is what I heard, come on," he said walking off. I pulled my bottom lip into my mouth and my eyes watered. Why would he do that? Damn, he was so fucking stubborn. I turned around and went to the girl's bathroom. I spotted the girl who I knew was afraid to sit in the lunchroom in her usual stall watching tv on her iPad. I knocked on the door, and she stared at me with scared eyes, like I was about to do something to her.

"I don't have any money on me or drugs," she quickly said. I shook my head.

"Can I please use your cell phone?" I said in one breath. She went into her clutch and pulled out a phone. She handed it to me and went back to her iPad. I called Ahmad, and the call was immediately sent to voicemail. I called him back three times until he finally picked up on the fourth ring.

"Who the fuck is this? I'm in class," he harshly whispered into the phone. I swear his voice was like music to my ears.

"Ahmad...it's me. Please come get me," I whispered.

I could hear shuffling then him sigh into the phone.

"Right now? What about your pops?"

"Fuck him. I have to see you. I can't go another day without you. It's been months," I replied feeling like I was about to lose my mind.

"Okay, I'mma call this phone when I'm outside and Pia…. I love you," he said. I felt like I could breathe normal after hearing his words.

"I love you too, so much," I said and ended the call. I discreetly wiped my eyes and stood by the stall door until Ahmad called me back which was thirty minutes later. I gave bathroom girl her phone back and quickly left out of the school. I spotted him in a black and red Range Rover. I smiled as I ran to the truck and got in. I looked at him and took in his appearance. He was rocking his hair in a curly taper that was lined to perfection. His beard had grown longer, and he was wearing sweats with J's on his feet. Ahmad was so fine he didn't have to go cash out on name brand clothes like that, but when he wanted to dress up, he did shut shit down.

"Damn girl, come here," he said and leaned over to kiss me gently on the lips. I held his face and kissed him harder as my eyes watered. I cried as our tongues tangled together. Damn, this was what we needed.

"I missed the fuck out of you," he said against my lips. He wiped my tears and smiled at me. I gazed into his eyes and continued to cry. It had only been four weeks, but it felt like it had been a lifetime since we had seen each other.

"Where are we going, Pia? I don't wanna make shit harder on you at home. I love you, but I don't wanna give him more reasons to keep you away from me," he said. I shrugged. I wasn't sure where we would go.

"Ahmad, I can't go back there and not be able to call or see you. It's hell," I complained.

Ahmad let my face go, and he sat back in his seat. He ran his hands over his head, and I smiled at him.

"What is that?"

Ahmad looked down and for a minute he looked a little embarrassed which was a first for him. He slowly showed me his right hand. On it was my name tattooed in cursive letters. I cheesed so hard it made my face hurt. I kissed his hand repeatedly until he decided to pull off.

"When did you get that?"

"A few weeks ago as a birthday gift to you. Shit, my mom's tried to take my damn head off and shit. She said we were moving too fast and that this time apart is what we need to grow as our own individual people. Do you feel like that?" he asked and glanced over at me. Just the thought of spending any more time apart from him made me nervous.

"No! I mean are old enough to know what we want Ahmad. I want you and I don't care about that stupid school fight or something as trivial as our age. I wanna be with you now," I told him never more sure of anything in my life. I knew I was whining to him, but it felt good to lay my worries down in his lap because I knew he would find a way to make things happen for us.

"Cool, because that's what I want too, ma. I came up with a way for us to be together. I just need to iron some shit out with my pops. I think I'mma go to school in North Carolina, Pia. Even though it's an Ivy League school, I know you can get in. Did you send your application?" he asked.

I sighed and stared out of the window.

"I did, but I didn't get it, Ahmad. I could just pay, but if I go against my dad, he might not give me the money," I laughed. "Hell, I know he won't if I choose to be with you," I said.

"Fuck the money I can pay it for you," he said as if it was nothing for him to pay my school tuition to an Ivy League college.

"Ahmad, I can't let you do that. I mean maybe I could just attend school here, and you come to visit me on the holidays," I suggested.

Ahmad shook his head as I noticed we were pulling up at his home. I frowned. I wasn't sure why we were here.

"Nah, I need you with me. I mean you can always apply to one of the colleges around there," he said, and I nodded because I could.

"Yeah, and I should be able to get in. I have a 3.8 GPA. I'm just looking for a school with a good dance program. You know I wanna open my studio up," I said as he parked.

"Yeah, and I know you will, ma. Look, I need for you to follow my lead in there. Okay?" he asked. I stared at him. What the hell was he up to?

"Okay…" I reluctantly said.

Ahmad flashed me his sexy smile and hopped out of the truck. He opened the door for me and pulled me into his arms. We hugged and kissed for a minute before he looked down at me.

"I'm doing this for us, Pia. So if shit gets heated just, please stick with me. I know how close you and my moms is, but it's gotta be us against the world. Okay?"

I licked my lips. Damn, I loved him.

"Okay."

He smiled and kissed me again.

"Bet, let's go," he said pulling me away.

Ahmad and I entered his house through the garage. We walked through the kitchen and found his parents laid out on the sofa with Aakil asleep on Ameer's lap. Ameer and Sophie glared at us with shocked expressions on their faces. Sophie was the first to speak.

"I see you two really wanna spend your whole school year on punishment. Pia, your father, doesn't want you over here and although I love you like a daughter, that might be for the best right now," she said looking at us. Ahmad grabbed my hand then pulled me by his side. I was so nervous I was damn near shaking.

"We're a year away from being eighteen and we decided to take control over our lives," he said confidently. Ameer glared at him with a smirk on his face.

"Oh, really? How do you plan on doing that when I'm still the person funding your fucking life?"

Ahmad cleared his throat.

"I know, and I appreciate you and mom for that. I have a proposition for you two. If I join the basketball team again can Pia and I get married?" he asked shocking his parents and me. Sophie quickly shook her head. She looked beautiful today in some black jeans, with a mustard colored turtleneck, and her hair flat ironed straight. Ameer was wearing one of his suits, and although they were lounging around, they looked so stylish doing something as simple as that.

"No....God, no, Ahmad. You're only seventeen. This is getting out of hand now. Pia, I'm about to take you home. You two are giving me fucking gray hair," she said standing up. I felt bad because I knew what we were putting them through it, but I couldn't help it. I needed to have Ahmad in my life.

"She's pregnant! I can't let my baby be born without me being her husband," Ahmad blurted out. My cheeks darkened, and I could feel my body heat rise. What the fuck was he doing? I had no idea he was about to say some crazy shit like this.

"She's what? Ameer!" Sophie yelled with watery, angry eyes. Ameer gently sat Aakil down and got up. Ahmad let my hand go, and Ameer grabbed him by the collar of his shirt. I stood by silently and watched Ameer stare into Ahmad's eyes. They looked so much alike, only Ahmad had hair and Ameer was taller and heavier than him.

"Say that one more time, Ahmad," he said through gritted teeth. Ahmad didn't flinch, but I did. I was afraid for him. I had never seen his dad look at him this way.

"Pops, Pia is carrying your grandchild. A *Matin*," he said and like déjà vu from the cemetery, Ameer started to choke him. This time, Sophie took her time walking over to them. She touched Ameer's arm as tears fell from her eyes. So much pain and anger radiated off of her and Ameer over something that wasn't even true. I felt like shit.

"Let him go. We have more things to worry about now. Like Angel," she murmured. It was then that my stomach started to hurt. I rushed out of the room, and ended up vomiting all over the floor in the hallway. I wasn't pregnant, hell I was still a virgin, but the thought of telling my dad this outrageous lie made me sick to my stomach.

"Ahmad, go help her since she is carrying your child. Your father and I will be back with Angel. I want you two to stay here," Sophie said.

Soon Ahmad was by my side. He cleaned up the hallway while I washed my face and used a new toothbrush to clean my mouth. I laid down in his bed, and he joined me thirty minutes later. We laid facing one another in silence. There was no guarantee my dad would make me go to

Mexico. We could have waited it out. I was a little upset with Ahmad for doing all of this.

"Ahmad," I sighed trying to think of the correct words to say. "Why the fuck did you do that?" I whispered.

Ahmad closed his eyes and placed his hands on my side. He stayed silent for a moment before speaking.

"This is the only way. After we get married, then we can just say you lost the baby. Don't you wanna be with me?" he asked in a somber tone. I nodded because I did but damn this was crazy.

"Ahmad, my dad. I don't want to hurt him. This is going to break his heart, and it's not even true!" I said. Ahmad sat up with me, and I turned my back to him. He wrapped his arms around me and kissed me on the neck. His scent was intoxicating as it wrapped around me like a blanket. I closed my eyes trying to calm myself down.

"Ahmad, I don't care about Portia, but my dad. He loves me, and he is going to hate me once they tell him this lie. We need to tell them the truth," I said to him.

He kissed my neck again and his hands slid down to my stomach.

"Pia, I would rather get you pregnant for real before telling them the truth. This time apart showed me that I can't live without you. They're the ones that pushed us together all those years ago. Shit, what the fuck did they expect to happen? I can't lose you, ma. Please don't tell them," he said speaking the last part into my neck. I nibbled on my bottom lip as I stared at the wall. What was I supposed to do? Break my dad's heart or Ahmad's? I knew Ahmad loved me, but he was wrong for putting me in this situation with him.

Chapter Nine

Pia

"No inheritance, no new clothes, no expensive ass dance school. No nothing!" he yelled pacing back and forth in front of me with red eyes. I pulled my knees to my chest as tears slipped from my eyes. I could beat the black off of Ahmad for doing this. I guess I was even crazier for going along with the shit.

"Se que papa," I said looking at him. He stopped walking and smirked at me.

"No need to speak it now since you plan on living your life with that fucking trash! I am so disappointed in you, Pia. How could you do this to yourself? Huh!" he yelled again making me jump.

"Right, I mean we knew you were having sex because no girl is a virgin at seventeen now, but Ahmad. Really? He's a lowlife drug dealer," Portia said and rolled her eyes. My dad and I both turned her way. Dressed in Versace from head to toe she looked very unbothered by the news that her daughter of seventeen years was soon to become a mother.

"Portia shut the fuck up," my dad said and turned back at me. My lips trembled as I looked at him.

"I'm so sorry, Dad. I promise it was a mistake, and I will graduate from high school and go to college."

"I know you will! Shit, I will kill that little nigga if you don't!" he yelled angrily. Portia even cowered a little under his tone. He was in rare form tonight. My brothers stood by the wall scowling. Primo looked more so shocked than anything, but Paulie was plain disappointed in me. He always said I would be dancing with some celebrity on their tour so I knew he thought that this would hold me back. If only he knew the truth.

"Angel, please calm down. I talked with Sophie, and she has a point. If they are in love and about to have a child, maybe we should consent to them getting married. At least then she'll have access to some of his money," Portia said I guess trying to make shit better. My dad glared at her, and a slow smile eased across his handsome face.

"You have two seconds to get the fuck out of this room," he said, and Portia broke her heel on her left shoe from running out of the room so fast. He turned back to me and shook his head. "I gave you everything, Pia. You are still a baby, yet you feel like you are old enough to bring a life into this world. My family wants to kill Ahmad. Do you know that a phone call could end his life?" he asked me.

"But I love him. And I would never forgive you!"

He turned around and walked over to my brothers. They talked quietly for a moment before he gave me his attention again.

"That might be a risk I'm willing to take. We're going to go talk with Ameer and his son. I will be back later, and if you leave this house, I promise you, you will never see his little ass again," he said and walked away with my brothers following after him.

Once they were out of the family room, Portia came back in with a glass of wine. She sat next to me, and rubbed my leg. I licked my lips and accidentally tasted some of my tears because I was crying again.

"Angel is just upset. He always thought you would be better than me, so that's why he's so mad. I mean you're a teen mom, but he has money so you didn't do that bad, it could be worse. He'll let the wedding happen to save face with his family, then you will be free to be with that boy of yours. You better make sure that baby calls me Portia. I'm too young to be a damn grandma," she said and finished her glass of wine.

*****

"The wedding will happen four weeks from now. Your father's family is flying in for it, and I pray no blood is shed. These men are itching to get violent," Sophie said as we walked into the hair salon. I nodded with so much on my mind. I had my dad on my mind heavy. Since he'd heard the fake news of the pregnancy, he'd said very little to me unless it was how disappointed he was with me. I knew Ahmad was just trying to keep us together, but I don't think he thought this shit through. I didn't want to admit it, but I could feel that my relationship with my dad may never be the same because of this lie.

"When do you go back to the doctor, Pia?" she asked, and I stopped walking. *Oh shit.*

"In five weeks," I quickly replied. Sophie nodded like that was a good timeframe, and we sat down. She sent some texts on her phone while I stared at Ahmad's text he'd just sent me.

Ahmad: *I wanna lick it when you get back ma.*

"Hey, Ma! How are you?" Rowan's snotty ass voice asked. Sophie and I both looked up. I had no idea she called her *ma.* That made me feel some kind of way. When it came to Ahmad, I had been spoiled. I felt like I was the only girl that was close to him and his family.

"Hi, Rowan," Sophie said rising. They gave each other a quick hug and Sophie sat back down with Rowan sitting next to her. My leg started to shake as I stared straight ahead. This bitch was trying me at the wrong time because I wasn't in the mood for her shit today.

"So how is your son doing? I been calling for him for days and he isn't picking up. I mean we had so much fun in New York, yet now he doesn't know who I am," Rowan said, and her eyes discreetly darted over towards me. Sophie and Rowan continued to talk. "When you all went to Vegas with me and my parents, things were good. What do you think happened, Ma?" she asked again.

When the fuck were, they taking all of these trips? I jumped up, no longer able to stay still, and Sophie looked at me, but my eyes were trained on Rowan's hoe ass. This bitch was looking at me with a very pleased look on her face.

"Oh, hey, Pia. Girl, I didn't even see you were there," she smiled at me and giggled. "I mean, it was like you were invisible; you know nonexistent. Not important, I could go on and on," she said laughing.

"Ahmad seems to think I'm important, and I never had to beg him to answer the phone."

Rowan stopped smiling.

"I'm sure you don't. He feels sorry for your dusty ass," she said, standing up.

Sophie stood up to stand in between us.

"Dusty? Just because I don't walk around looking like a slut doesn't mean I'm dusty."

Rowan smiled and flicked some of her hair over her shoulder.

"Humph, Ahmad seems to like it," she said and laughed.

I laughed with her. She was such a stupid bitch if she thought that ran through pussyof hers would get Ahmad. He didn't want that shit.

"Right, him asking me to marry him is his way of liking you," I said, and she looked at me with a blank look on her face. She turned to Sophie, and I started laughing at her dumb ass. "Pick up your jaw," I said through my laughter, and Sophie pulled me to her side.

"Pia and Ahmad are about to have a family and be married. This trivial shit doesn't matter anymore. Have a good day, Rowan. Pia, we'll just come back," Sophie said and pulled me away. She quickly rescheduled our appointments and we left.

"Pia, I'm telling you this because I love you. If you want to be with Ahmad, you're going to have to get some tough skin. Rowan is only the beginning, especially since he's going to the NBA. These chicks don't care. There will always be someone out there looking to take your place. As long as your foundation at home is good, then you won't have to worry about anything. I hate that you and Ahmad are so young, but I can tell you two have a strong bond. That's a good thing. Work to make it's strong as it can be, and trust and believe no woman or man will be able to tear you two apart," Sophie said as we walked to her truck. I smiled. I swear she always gave the best advice.

"But Ameer seems so perfect, and he loves you so much," I said to her, getting into the truck. Sophie laughed.

"Pia, no relationship is perfect. I could write a book on the things I went through with Ameer. However, we made it through, and I still feel like taking his head off at times, but I love him," she replied. As she pulled off, I thought of his real mom, Tatum. I knew it was a touchy subject for everyone in his family, but I still had questions, and I knew Sophie would be truthful with me.

"Has Ameer talked to Ahmad anymore about his mom Tatum?"

Sophie took a deep breath before sighing.

"No, he hasn't. I don't want this to pull my family apart, Pia. Ahmad isn't going to be satisfied until he knows everything that happened to her, but sometimes the truth is more than we can bare. I'm praying on how to handle it. I'm dealing with very headstrong men. All of the Matin men are stubborn as hell," she said shaking her head. I smiled thinking of my own Matin man. Hell, look what he had me agreeing to do just so that we could be together. Some old outlandish shit.

"After the marriage, you and Ahmad will stay in the guest house until college. I'm thinking that with you being pregnant maybe you should stay with me until you have the baby. I don't want you having to raise a child alone. Ahmad will be very busy with school and basketball. You could always go see him and vice versa. It wouldn't have to be forever," she suggested. I didn't like the sound of that at all. The whole point of the marriage was for us to be together.

"But then we'll be living apart, Ma."

Sophie glanced over at me with her beautiful face and shrugged.

"Baby you have to sacrifice sometimes. I want to help with my grandbaby, and I can't do that with you staying in another state. I think this is best for all of us. Just think about it, please," she replied. I nodded, but wasn't even considering staying apart from Ahmad. I wasn't pregnant anyway.

When we got back to the house, the driveway was lined with cars. Sophie smiled as she spotted her sisters standing near the front door, letting their kids go in first.

"Pia, get used to them being around all of the time. They all act like my house is the damn family home. Come on, baby," she said and got out of the truck. I licked my semi-dry lips and got out. Ahmad stood off to the side of the house with his cousin Mauri and his friends. He waved me over and while Sophie went after her sisters, I went to him. I was dressed down in jeans with a collared pink polo while two girls stood by with leggings on and tank tops showing off their camel toes and every fucking thing while they eye fucked Mauri. Yes, he was a big time NBA player, but I didn't look at him that way. To me, he was just family.

"Hey, Pia," Mauri said walking towards me. I smiled and gave him a quick hug.

"Hey, Mauri! Where's Jess and the kids?" I asked stepping back. Mauri looked down at me with those honey-colored eyes of his and smiled. Damn, he was fine as hell, but I would never let Ahmad know that.

"They in the house. You know her pregnant ass in there sleep," he replied. His wife was four months pregnant with a girl, and we were all ready to see her beautiful little self. Jess was gorgeous, so I knew their daughter would be a doll.

"Aww, I'll have to go see her," I said as Ahmad glanced me over with those eyes of his. Maybe because we'd known each other for so long, I could tell what he was thinking and vice versa. I could see that he was horny as hell, and I would have been cool with giving him a hand job but after finding out he had been vacationing with Rowan, I didn't have nothing for his ass.

"Pia, I thought you was getting your hair done. Why your shit looks the same, Ugly," he said dribbling the ball. I stepped away from Mauri and walked over to him. Ahmad tossed the ball to me, and I threw it back at him. He and I played ball for a few minutes. I even made a few shots.

"Damn, Pia out here flexing on you," Mauri said watching us play. Mauri and Ahmad's groupies had walked off once they noticed no one was paying attention to their asses.

"Man…cuz you know what it is. I taught Pia how to play," Ahmad said and made a shot from the other end of the court. I rolled my eyes at his show off ass. He looked at me and smirked. "Don't hate, Pia. That's not a good look on you," he said chuckling.

I chuckled with him.

"You know what else is not a good look? Rowan walking up on me and ma in the hair salon and telling me about how you two went on all of these vacations together," I replied.

He pulled that stupid ass bottom lip of his in between his teeth, and his head fell back. A clear sign that he was thinking of a lie to say.

"Pia, we went to Vegas, and she was there with her family. I saw her one time when I was in New York with my uncle Kasam while he performed. I spoke and kept it moving," he said, not looking me in the eyes. He could never look at me when he was lying.

"Yeah, whatever," I said and walked off. I wasn't about to listen to those bullshit ass lies.

"Pia, take it easy on him," Mauri said as I walked past him. I kept on walking and could feel Ahmad's presence behind me. He followed me into the house that was filled with his family. We walked into the kitchen, and his mom and aunts looked at both of us. Drew, his youngest aunt, smiled. She was cute with a feisty attitude to her.

"What he did do now, Pia?" she asked me, holding a drink in her hand.

I smiled, but on the inside, I was upset because for him to lie to me proved to me that he was hiding something. He probably fucked her in Vegas and New York when he claimed to have been missing me. I didn't usually go to them when he made me mad, but I wanted they opinion on it.

"I was at the hair salon with Ma and his ex-girlfriend Rowan walked up to us."

Drew rolled her eyes.

"I always disliked that little fast ass girl. She was twelve staring down Aamil and shit. I told Sophie I was gonna end up whooping her little ass," she said, making Sophie laugh.

"Drew, she's a kid," Sophie said to her.

Drew looked at Sophie.

"Have you seen her? That little bitch is not a fucking kid anymore. Those hips, ass, and titties show me she been doing some very grown up shit, and she won't be doing it with my husband. Not saying he would ever look her way, but that won't stop her from trying," Drew replied.

"Baby, don't put my name in shit. Ahmad is the one that's in trouble, not me so chill out," his uncle Aamil said walking into the kitchen looking so damn good. Aamil, unlike Ahmad, was dark with dark brown eyes, silky black hair that was cut low to his head along with the Matin men signature long beard. He smiled at me before going over to Drew and hugging her. She buried her face into his shirt, and he looked Ahmad's way. Ahmad was behind me all quiet shit because he knew he had been caught.

"Ahmad, you not even thinking about that girl is you?" Aamil asked.

"Unk, you already know I'm not. I don't know why Pia even in here tripping then your wife and her sisters getting Pia worked up for nothing," he replied, making his auntie and mom look his way with raised brows.

"Pia, you gone need to whoop her ass and Ahmad's," Erin, his other aunt said, looking at me. I laughed because I knew she was dead serious.

"See what I'm talking about? Kasam! Come get your wife!" Ahmad yelled.

Sophie and her sisters laughed, Aamil even chuckled.

"Man, y'all doing too much. Rowan is nothing to me. Pia knows I love her," Ahmad said and hugged me from the back. Usually, his mom would tell him to cut it out, but I guess since they thought I was pregnant this was acceptable now.

"Well love her enough not to fuck up," Drew said pulling away from her husband to look at Ahmad.

"I will Auntie," he replied and pulled us away.

We went upstairs to his bedroom, and he locked his bedroom door while I took off my shoes and jeans. Ahmad slapped me on my butt, and I hit his arm. I was in no mood to be playing with him.

"Don't touch me."

"*Don't touch me*," he mimicked me as I climbed into the bed. I rolled my eyes and got all the way on one end while he climbed in behind me. He hugged me from the back while I closed my eyes.

"I didn't take no trips with her, Pia. I promise you I didn't. You know she is only doing this shit to get at you, and you fall for it every time," he whispered in my ear. I ignored him. I wasn't trying to hear shit he had to say because I felt like he was lying.

"Pia, so you just gone not fucking talk to me? I don't give no fucks about that girl. Never have and I never will," he said, letting me go. Soon I heard his bedroom door open and close. I wanted to believe Ahmad, but Rowan seemed to be someone that was always there. I'd given up a lot to be with him and if I was found out he was seeing her behind my back, I just might kill him and her ass.

Chapter Ten

Ahmad

Ahmad, this is your grandma. I hate that I had to find you on here, but I had no choice. Your father refuses to allow for any of us to see you. We love you and whenever you're ready we will be here for you. Were your family as well. Please call me I'm back in Michigan for good…313-779-4000

I shook my head thinking about the message. I was shocked as fuck to wake up to my grandma trying to contact me on the internet. My pops' mom and dad were gone so this was the only living grandparent I had and on some real shit, I wanted to meet up with them. I just needed to do it at the right time.

Right now I had to get this shit with Pia and me together. What she didn't know was that I very much planned on getting her pregnant on our wedding night. It wasn't to trap her or no shit like that. More so as a way to solidify our unity. Basketball was my world, but so was Pia. I needed both of them in my life, and if we had a baby together, then I would go even harder on the court.

Yeah, my pops had money so essentially I did too, but I wanted to make my own millions. He made it clear from the jump that I could never go to the streets, but the reality was if

I wanted to I could. My uncles Aamil's and Kadar's pops was the fucking plug. He would never tell me no. Hell, he called me his grandson and shit. At the end of the day, none of them would, but for now I was going to try to do this shit the right way. The kind of way that could keep that beautiful smile on my mom's face and shit. Like right now I was with her at the nail salon. All of these old bitches in here checking me out while I'm trying to get in quality time with my day one.

"So Ma, you looking beautiful today with your hair all done up," I said and winked at her. My mom's smiled. The reality was that she was beautiful every day I just neglected to tell her most of the time. The way she stepped up to say Pia could move in with us after the wedding showed just much she loved me, although I already knew she did.

"Thank you, Ahmad," she said. I sat back in my seat ignoring how sexy the fucking nail technician was. Mercy was a cold ass piece of work. I had been lusting after her and her twin for years.

"Ma, I got this message on the book from my grandma, Tatum's mother, saying she wanna meet me and shit. I mean stuff. What you think about that?"

My mom sighed. I could tell this was tough for her, but damn shouldn't it be about me and not about how her and my pops felt about the situation.

"Ahmad, I think you should do it. I want you to know all of your family. All I ask is that you remember the truth.

What you know and not what someone else tells you," she replied. I kissed her soft cheek.

"Ma, nobody could ever make me think any less of you. You have been taking care of me since I was a child. You are my momma," I told her looking at her.

"This is too much for me. Sophie y'all about to have me crying in here," Mercy said and dapped her eye. My mom did shed a tear or two. She looked at me with glassy eyes.

"Don't ever forget that either Ahmad. I love you, and you are my son," she said. I nodded and winked at her. There was nothing anyone would ever be able to tell me about this woman. I loved her ass too much.

"Ma what happened with Rowan and Pia at the salon?" I asked since it was still fresh on my mind. I had been kissing Pia's ass since it happened just to get her to talk to me. Finally, we were back on speaking terms and shit had been good between us.

"Ahmad, that girl is trouble. Her sneaky little ass came over talking about these trips and trying to say shit to hurt Pia. I wished Pia wasn't pregnant so that she could have beat her ass," she said making Mercy laugh. Mercy looked at us.

"Pregnant? You about to be a grandma Sophie?"

My ma smiled proudly. I thought she would have gotten emotional. I knew she was upset with me still.

"Yes. This son of mine got his girlfriend pregnant, and they're getting married," she replied. Mercy looked from me to my mom.

"I wish you two the best Ahmad. Things happen, but that's life. Just trust in the Lord and you will get through it," she said sincerely. I nodded that was real of her.

"Thanks, beautiful," I said making my ma smack her lips.

Mercy looked at me with them damn green eyes of hers.

"You a mess boy and too damn handsome. Don't put that sweet girl through no bull," she warning me and went back to my mom's nails.

"Trust me, he won't," my ma said giving me a stern look. I raised my hands in the air making my watch fall slightly down my wrist.

"Ma, you know I won't. I'mma handle Rowan," I told her.

"You better, Ahmad. She's trouble, and if you keep messing with her little ass, she will ruin everything you have with Pia. Pia loves you, but I don't take her as the type to be a doormat," she said.

"I know, and I'm done with Rowan," I said looking straight ahead.

"You should be. You're about to be married and have a kid. Let that girl go," she said and started talking with Mercy.

"Ahmad no," Rowan said, and I pushed her head back down. Pia was in Chicago with her mom, and I was at Rowan's hitting it from the back. I loved Pia with all of my fucking heart, but I had needs. Yes, foreplay was cool, but I needed to cum from fucking. That hand shit was for the birds.

"Ummm…. baby yes," Rowan moaned. I closed my eyes and imagined it was Pia I was sliding in and out of. Her silky soft skin beneath my fingers. Her long hair draped onto her back all sweated out and shit. I could feel my nut coming up quick, so I hit it harder.

"Shit," I grunted and went in so deep Rowan had to bite down onto her cover, so she didn't scream out. I came deep in the condom before pulling out. I knew who I wanted to be with and having a kid by anyone other than Pia was not an option so for these broads I always strapped up.

"Damn, girl," I said with Pia still on my mind. I flushed the condom down the toilet and then washed my shit off. Rowan laid on her bed as I walked back into her spacious bedroom. If Pia wasn't my girl, Rowan would be it. I did have some feelings for her, but it didn't compare to Pia. Pia was the one for me. I knew it from the moment I saw her plain looking ass, but that's what I loved about Pia. She didn't give a fuck about trends. She was comfortable with being herself. That was good enough for her, and I loved that because her being herself was the sexiest shit to me in the world.

"So this is what we'll be doing when you get married? Sneaking around to fuck because your precious little princess can't do the dick right?" Rowan asked. I smirked at her.

"Keep running that big ass mouth of yours and you won't have to worry about ever sucking this dick again. You talk too fucking much, and nobody likes a sneaky bitch so stop with that shit Rowan," I said glaring at her ass.

Rowan stopped smiling immediately.

"Ahmad, I was just playing with her," she whined. I slipped on my basketball shorts.

"Well, I'm not fucking playing with you. If you even look my bitch way, it's a wrap on us. Shit, if you out and you see me, and her somewhere don't even fucking think about us, or it's a wrap on you," I told her. Rowan pulled the covers up over her body.

"I loved you before she did. I've always loved you. Why don't you love me back?"

I grabbed my car keys. I wasn't a cold hearted nigga. I wasn't looking to break her heart, but I had to be real with her. A relationship is something we would never have again. Shit, the one we had didn't work because of Pia. It was obvious she was the one I couldn't be without.

"Look, I got love for you. I been knowing you my whole fucking life and shit, but Pia is.... just Pia. I love the fuck out of that girl and if that's too much for you to handle than lose my number. She's gonna always be the most important lady in my life. I gotta go," I told her and walked out of her bedroom. I left her house and got into my car. I rode with the music off with my mind on Pia. She had been gone a day, and I was already missing her big headed ass.

I pulled up to my house and spotted my pops getting into his Range. I parked next to him, and he called me over to his truck. I got in and was immediately hit with some grade "A" ass weed smoke. He backed out of the driveway as he ran one hand over his bald head. This nigga here was my fucking hero for real. I respected no one more than I did him.

"Coming from Rowan's place, huh?" he asked driving down the road. I sat back smiling. This nigga knew my every fucking move and shit. I was starting to wonder if he had his right-hand nigga who I considered an uncle, Luke, on me.

"Something like that."

He laughed.

"Nigga, I'm not Pia. Don't bullshit me. You have to wrap up that shit with Rowan. Sophie told me how she outed you at the beauty shop and shit. Pia is who you wanna be with so act like it. Fucking around will only leave you fucked in the end. I knew this was too much for you Ahmad you just too selfish to let Pia go," he said which was kind of truthful, but shit he was no better than me. I heard about all the shit he did to get with my moms. Burning her damn apartment down and shit so that she could live with him. How was that not worse than what the fuck I was doing?

"But, Pops I'm not married yet. Once we say I do, I'm done with Rowan's ass." My pops looked at me with the same fucking eyes as mine and chuckled.

"If you say so. All I'm saying is that Pia got your heart and your baby. She's soon to be your wife. This is the fucking situation you put yourself in, so step up to the plate and handle it like a man."

My nose flared. What the fuck was he saying?

"Dad, I am a man."

He looked over at me as he pulled up to his jeweler's house. He parked in his winding driveway and cleared his throat.

"Look, Ahmad. I'm far from fucking perfect but with my kids, I tried to be. I like Pia, I do, but I didn't want this for you so soon. You all both young as hell and you might think it's easy to just cut off Rowan and them other chicks you fucking with, but lust and immaturity is a motherfucka. Jumping into a life you not ready for can be bad for all the people involved. All of that pain and heartache Pia might experience can be avoided," he said to me.

My heart started to beat fast because he was pissing me the fuck off. I trusted his judgment and all, but for him to try to tell me how to take care of Pia was bullshit. I knew Pia better than I knew myself. As long as I had breath in my body, she was going to be with me and rest assured she would be good.

"What I'm saying is that if you not ready for this let me know, and we can call it off. Fuck Angel on some for real shit. I don't want Pia, Angel or even Sophie to put this pressure on you. A baby doesn't mean love or marriage. Don't force it if it's not there, Ahmad. Regardless, Pia and her child will be okay," he said looking over at me for a response. I hated how parent's automatically felt like everything fucking thing they said was right. This nigga had fucked up plenty of times, yet he wanted to be all holier than though with me and shit. Trying to tell me not to be pressured into something. Nobody could ever make me do something I didn't want to do not even him.

"Pops, I love her. From the moment you made me watch her I liked her. I wanna always have her in my life as my woman. I'll never love another chick the way I love her, and that's real," I told him earnestly.

"But you only seventeen. How the fuck do you even know what love is?"

I smiled at him. People always had a way of walking themselves into some bullshit.

"The same way Ma did when she met you at nineteen and took on being a parent to a son that wasn't even hers. She took a chance on you like how Pia is taking a chance on me. That's fucking love Pops," I said making him smirk at me.

He started laughing and opened his truck door.

"Your little ass think you know it all, huh? Okay, don't ever say I didn't try to stop you. Now come on," he said. We got out of the truck, walked up to Eric's house, and hit his doorbell. He had been cool with my pops for years, and he owned a slew of jewelry stores along with pawn shops. He was a cool ass nigga.

"Aww, shit royalty is on my doorstep," he said opening the front door. My pops chuckled and gave him some dap. I followed suit, and we went into his house. He led us into his dining room, and his table was covered with a black suede cloth. On top of the cloth was some of the most freaked out jewelry I had ever seen. I zeroed in on a princess cut ring with a pink diamond. I picked it up as my pops, and Eric chopped it up.

"Ahmad getting married? What the fuck is going on over there Ameer? I expect that kind of stuff from my family but you? You making him do it already," Eric said laughing.

"This all on him nigga. He got her pregnant, so he's doing what he has to do," he replied, but he wasn't laughing. I felt kind of fucked up because I knew he was upset with me. Still, this needed to be done. There really wasn't no other way to keep my bae with me.

"Dad, I want this one for her," I said and handed him the ring. He nodded as he looked down at it.

"Yeah, this shit nice. Eric, Sophie told me she texted you Pia's ring size and also let me get that tennis bracelet for my baby," he said with a smile finally gracing his face. Only ma could make him smile like that and what he didn't get was that Pia had that same fucking effect on me. I couldn't function without her ass. Yeah, I might entertain Rowan and a few other bitches from time to time, but they would never be Pia. That was a bar they would never reach.

"And I'm the one that's whipped," I said laughing. My pops and Eric both laughed.

"Shit what Sophie put on me, Pia ain't gone be doing for at least ten more years. That's that grown woman shit," he said and slapped hands with Eric. They walked off, and I sat down at the table. I had a lot of shit to handle in a short amount of time, but all I could think about was finally sliding into my baby and making her a Matin.

Chapter Eleven

Pia

"Here get this," Portia said holding a black G-string in the air. The last thing I wanted to do was go lingerie shopping with her.

"No, that's not classy," I said, and she laughed at me.

"Classy? You think Ahmad's little fine ass looking for something classy, Pia? He's looking for the freaky stuff sweetie. He's seventeen, not thirty-eight," she said and walked away. I rolled my eyes and decided to check on Ahmad. I had created an account to follow Rowan on IG. I knew it was silly, but still, it put my mind at ease. I scrolled through her photos and yeah Ahmad was in some, but he was always with a gang of people. There was, however, one picture of her in bed, and she'd taken a picture of herself in some basketball shorts. The same basketball shorts that Ahmad owned. The picture was only a day old, and the caption read, "*bae shit so big on me.*" I wasn't sure if they were his or what but I was damn sure going to find out.

"Pia, come here!" Portia's ghetto ass yelled across the store. I put my phone away and walked over to her. I wanted to go dress shopping with Sophie, but Portia had already picked me out a form fitting mermaid gown, and now she was buying me lingerie. I was beyond irritated and ready to go home.

"You don't have to wear white since you pregnant anyway, but that white set is too cute to pass up. In a minute you're going to be big as a fucking house. Let's woo him now while you're still appealing to the eye," she said handing me a one piece that had the nipple and crotch area cut out. I frowned looking it over. It wasn't that it was ugly it was just weird that my mom would give me that then it reminded me too much of some shit she would wear for one of her men. I'd seen some images of her that I just couldn't get out of my brain. Plus, look at how fucked up they treat her. I didn't want Ahmad to treat me like some low life hoe because I dressed the part.

"Okay whatever," I said knowing she wasn't going to let up until I agreed to get what she wanted me to have.

"Good!" she said and walked away. My phone buzzed as Porta purchased my stuff. I pulled it out and looked at it.

Xerius: *So I heard about the baby and engagement. I guess congrats are in order.*

Me: *thanks…*

Xerius: *that nigga that scared to lose you? he must know I'mma snatch your beautiful ass up the minute I can…*

Me: *Xerius stop playing*

Xerius: *ha-ha…you got it but who said I was playing? He got your heart right now, but bets believe I'm chasing that motherfucka…*

Me: *Goodbye Xerius…*

Xerius: *bye beautiful I miss you…take it easy*

I put my phone away smiling. I looked up, and Portia was all in my damn face.

"Ahmad got you smiling. It's good to see he makes you happy," she said before walking away. A tinge of guilt rushed through me considering it was Xerius who'd made me smile, but it was just a text. I loved and wanted to be with Ahmad. Shit, I was risking everything to have him so Xerius could try all he wanted but my heart was with the man I was about to marry.

After picking up my shoes and jewelry, we went back to Portia's place. I was headed to my room when her newest boyfriend stopped me. He was a local rapper with a rap sheet as long as his tall ass body. His name was Choppa, and he was already getting on my fucking nerves.

"How old are you again?" he asked with a blunt hanging from his mouth. I rolled my eyes and moved around him. He tried to grab my arm and I pushed his hand away.

"Choppa stop. Her fucking father would end you, nigga, plus you need to be in that room with me using that mouth of yours," Portia said walking behind him. I cringed on the inside. Portia had no tact whatsoever. She called it sexual freedom I called it being a hoe.

"Oh yeah? I'm trying to see what your daughter on? She down with her sexy ass?" He asked, and I sped up my pace. I practically ran to my room and closed the door before I could hear her reply. I locked it and even placed my powder pink chair behind the knob so that no one could even turn it. I sat on my bed and Face-Time, Ahmad.

"I miss you, Ugly," he said answering. He looked at my face, and his smile went away. He was laying down in his bed with Aakil asleep beside him.

"What's wrong?"

I sighed not sure if I should tell him. Someone started knocking on my door, and I sat my phone down.

"Yes!" I yelled out.

"Pia, he was just playing so there is no need to go be a snitch. You know I would never let anyone do anything to you. Choppa was high, and that's it. I made him leave baby," Portia yelled back. She seemed worried like she was afraid my dad would whoop her ass or something. I rubbed my eyes tired of going through the motions with her. Every time I came here, it was something.

"Whatever Portia," I yelled back and took Ahmad's call off of Facetime. I didn't want him to see my flushed cheeks or teary eyes. It wasn't that I was afraid of Choppa. Just being here was a reminder of the piss poor excuse of a mother I had. I didn't need for her to be perfect but she could at least be decent. She was so reckless and selfish.

"Pia, what the fuck is going on?" Ahmad asked as I laid down on my side.

"Nothing. Portia has some dude named Choppa over here, and he was just pissing me off. I'm okay, though."

"Are you sure? I'll come up there," he said like Chicago was around the corner. I smiled at how much I loved him.

"No, it's cool, really it is. I wish I had something of yours here so that I could at least smell you. Like them basketball shorts that I love so much," I said thinking about the shorts I'd seen on Rowan's IG. He got quiet, and I regretted taking that damn FaceTime off.

"Shit, I just wish I had you here. I'm horny bae," he said in a low voice. My body tingled at his admission.

"I wanna be able to handle that for you, Ahmad," I said feeling slightly uncomfortable, but I couldn't let him know that. Portia made me second guess myself and all of my thoughts. I knew that I wanted to lose my virginity to him, but my biggest fear was giving him something so precious only for him to still run out and see other girls. That would break my heart. I valued my body and my love because it was something very special and if Ahmad wanted it, he was going to have to value it too.

"I want you to handle it too. My dick getting hard just from you talking like that. We gone play when you get back?" he asked in reference to us giving each other oral sex or in my case a hand job. My pussy tingled at the thought of him touching it again.

"Yeah, we can."

"With our mouths, this time, ma, okay," he quickly added in. I wasn't sure about that, but I didn't want to kill the moment, so I agreed.

"Okay, Ahmad."

"Bet, that promise well get me through this next day without you. I wanna kiss them pretty ass lips of yours Pia…shit I wanna kiss both of them," he said making my stomach flutter with butterflies.

"Ahmad, get off the phone," Sophie said in the background. He chuckled while I held in my laugh. I know she was tired as hell of us at the moment.

"Pia, let me talk to my moms I'll call you back," he said and ended the call.

My phone rang before I could sit it down and I answered it. The call was blocked.

"Hello…"

The other end of the phone was silent. I looked at my phone again and saw the call had ended. I rolled my eyes and put my phone away. I hadn't talked to Zaria since the fight, so maybe she had moved on to harassing me now. Whatever the case was I didn't have time for it.

*****

Three days later I sat with my dad inside of a popular Japanese restaurant in Troy. He was deciding what to order while I studied him. In my eyes, he was like the perfect man. He was handsome, loyal and smart. Everything I saw in Ahmad. My dad had done an amazing job at raising me, and I didn't want him to feel like it was all in vain. I planned on making him very proud of me one day.

"I wanna dance at this new school dad."

He stared at me with eyes the color of Columbian coffee and he smiled. Dressed in a three-piece steel gray suit, he was the best looking man in the room.

"Really? How do you plan on dancing with a baby in your stomach? No ballet or hip hop sets for you," he said and went back to his menu. I swallowed the lump in my throat. I wasn't fucking pregnant, but I knew I couldn't tell him that just yet.

"I know, but I can always do it after the baby. They're really good and even sometimes dance with celebrities."

He nodded but didn't say anything. He cleared his throat as he looked at me.

"Pia, I can't sit and pretend to be happy. You getting married and having his baby is equivalent to picking up a knife and stabbing me through the heart. You've gutted me baby worse than Portia ever could. Maybe you are your mother's daughter," he said and casually took a sip of his drink. I looked away from him as quickly as I could. For him to even compare me to Portia was a slap in the face. He gutted me with that statement because I would never fucking be like her.

I couldn't believe he was being so cruel to me. I'd dressed up just for him. I was wearing a black high neck skater dress with black Louboutin flats, and my hair was in loose waves. I was trying to spend quality time with him, but as long as he thought I was pregnant, I wasn't sure if that could happen.

"So the wedding is a week away now and yet you don't even have a fucking ring. This is so nice," he said sarcastically. I looked at him and held in my smart remarks. I knew I would get a ring. That type of stuff didn't move me. I loved Ahmad and if he were as broke as the people asking for change, I still would. My love for him wasn't conditional.

"Dad, he'll get me a ring," I said sighing. He smiled.

"Ah, I'm sure he will. So how is his family? Has Olivia been okay?" he asked finally placing the menu on the table. Olivia was Ahmad's aunt and someone my dad had dated. He asked about her here and there. I could tell a part of him wished they were together although she was married to Ahmad's uncle Kadar and had a family with him.

"She's good. Omari is really big too. He looks so much like her with those eyes," I said smiling. My dad chuckled.

"I'm sure he does. Does he look anything like Kadar?" he asked. I immediately nodded because he did. I was trying to spare my dad's feelings, but I see he was in the mood to get them hurt.

"Yes, like his twin," I said praying that would be enough for him to finally let Olivia completely go. She never even asked me about him. Actually, none of them did except for Sophie, and I knew she only did it to be nice. She was sweet like that.

"Hmph," he grunted and soon the waitress was taking our orders. My dad dropped the subject of Olivia, and we got to enjoy the rest of our lunch together.

Chapter Twelve

Ahmad

"Fuck! Get that shit, Ro!" I moaned as she went to town on me. My legs buckled, and I fell back onto the bed. I set out to grab some shit from the mall and meet Pia at my place later on. Rowan texted me *sixty-nine*, and I met up with her at her sister's spot who was a flight attendant. I was a week away from getting married, so I was trying to get Rowan out of my system. She was sucking the life out of my dick and because I knew Pia wasn't gonna do it, even though she told me she would, I was trying to treat myself. I loved Pia, but I knew when her ass was lying, and she was not about to top a nigga off. She just wasn't.

"Mmmm…fuck…right there," I said and guided her head up and down onto my shaft. Rowan sucked me so good my damn vision started to blur. I knew she was doing the most because I told her this would be the last time. She was trying to make me re-think my shit and a weaker nigga definitely would have.

"Fuck, I'm cumming," I said, and she pulled back. She held out her tongue, and I came right on it. She gargled my shit and spat it right back on the length of my dick before sucking it right back up. The visual of her beautiful ass doing all of that made me weak. I fell back and took a deep breath. This bitch got on my fucking nerves. Who taught her how to suck dick like that? That shit was ridiculous.

"Ahmad, you taste so fucking good, daddy," she said in this sexy ass voice as she straddled me. She started to grind on my lap, and my dick got back instantly hard. I felt her rising, and I used the little bit of strength I had to push her ass off of me.

"Ahmad! Damn," she said getting up off of the floor. The fall wasn't even that hard, so I don't know why she was even tripping.

"Rowan, don't even try no sneak shit like that again," I said and grabbed a condom off of the nightstand. Rowan took it from me and climbed back onto my lap. She opened it with her teeth and slowly slide it on my dick.

"I was just playing," she lied, staring down at me. I smirked and raised her up so that she could take me for a quick ride. I had shit to do, and she was holding a nigga up.

"Damn…you feel so big," she moaned and arched her back. She placed her hands flat on my chest and started popping that pussy all over me. Rowan and I had been fucking since we were eleven, so we both knew each other's bodies, but I wasn't the only nigga she fucked with, and she wasn't the only girl I had sexed.

"Damn girl," I said smacking her ass. Rowan's head fell back, and her perky titties bounced in the air. I moved around so I could pull one of her fat nipples into my mouth. I was gonna miss the fuck out of this pussy.

Two hours later I rushed into my house and ran right into my little sister Soraya. She was ten going on thirty and shit. I loved her little spoiled ass, though.

"Where you been at? And who were you around that smell like Prada Candy?" she asked with her hand on her hip. Her little ass had on a black outfit with her small brown and pink Gucci flats and the purse to match. My pops had created a little monster with her spoiled ass. I chuckled looking down at her.

"Man, take your little ass on somewhere," I said and pushed her out of the way.

"Pia waiting on you!" she yelled after me. I slowed down and sniffed my shirt. Shit, did I smell like Prada Candy?

"Hey, baby! Pia yelled running towards me. I wished I could have fucking showered at least, but of course, I couldn't turn her away. I opened my arms and hugged her tightly. She pulled back after a minute and looked me over.

"You smell different," she said frowning at me. I smiled. That bitch Rowan must have sprayed me with her perfume.

"Soraya's ass just sprayed me with her purse spray and shit," I lied. Pia gave me the up and down and smiled. She was looking good as hell in her skinny jeans and cream shirt and her hair were on point as usual. I took a step back and licked my lips.

"Ma took me to the salon," she said and spun around. She had gotten her hair layered, and it was hanging down her back. I liked it, it was a sexy ass style on her. I grinned as I walked to her and gently yanked on her hair. I couldn't wait to pull that shit from the back. I was so used to her hair being wavy and pulled back in a bun. I pulled her into my arms and slapped her ass.

"I can't wait to sweat that shit out," I whispered in her ear before sticking my tongue in it.

"Ahmad!" Aakil yelled running towards us. I let Pia go and picked his little bad ass up. My ma walked down the hallway after him in some tight ass yoga shorts and a sports bra. She had her hair pulled back away from her face.

"Little boy come here so I can take you home," she said grabbing him out of my arms. I looked her up and down with a frown. She was showing way too much skin for my liking. I had to lump so many niggas up because of the slick shit they would say about my moms.

"Ma where you going with that on? Pops know you wearing this?" I asked shaking my head at her fit.

Ma waved her hand in the air as Meelah came down the hallway followed by Soraya. They were all wearing workout gear and shit.

"Were going to the gym for a while. Y'all be good, and Ahmad clean that dirty ass room of yours," she said and walked off. I smiled. Hell yeah, a few hours without them was what I needed. I was a little drained because of Rowan's ass, but I could at least lick on my baby and make her feel good. Shit, she deserved it, coming here looking that damn beautiful.

"Come on Pia, let's go clean my room," I smirked pulling her away.

"Ahmad, I can't stay too late. My dad gave me a ten o'clock curfew since my uncles are here for the wedding," she said following me. I chuckled. Angel was a bitch ass nigga. He let her stay every night all last week, now he wanted to front for his peoples like he had shit on lock. Yeah, okay.

Pia and I went into my junky ass bedroom, and while I took off my clothes, Pia pulled her long ass hair back and started to clean up.

"Pia, can you go make me something to eat, too bae?" I asked walking towards the bathroom.

"…. Yes, Ahmad," she said like I was working her nerves. I smiled and went into the bathroom. I shut the door and took my clothes off before jumping in the shower. I made sure to wash my shit good before getting out. After drying off, I went back into the bedroom, and I had a plate of ma's good ass spaghetti sitting on my nightstand. Pia was sitting on the bed with her back to me looking down at her phone. My stomach grumbled at the smells that were coming off of the plate.

"Thanks, bae, I'm hungry as hell," I said sitting down. I looked around and noticed her ass hadn't really cleaned my room, but I decided to let it slide. I didn't wanna argue with her, I would just clean the rest of the shit myself, but Pia knew what was up. She knew I didn't like to clean up anything. I said a quick prayer and grabbed my fork. I started to eat my food and spotted a fucking gold condom wrapper on my damn plate with some spaghetti wrapped around it. I snatched that shit and turned around.

"Pia, what the fuck is this?"

Pia stood and spun around. Her eyes were swollen from crying, and she was holding a damn steak knife.

"Ahmad, I'mma ask you this one time. Are you cheating on me?" she asked slowly walking around the bed. I quickly put my plate down. This was why I didn't want her associating with my mom and aunts for too long. I walked to her and grabbed her wrist that was holding the knife. Fuck type of shit was she on?

"Pia, give me this fucking knife," I said, twisting her wrist. With her free hand, she mushed the shit out of my fucking face.

"I swear I knew them was your shorts! You still fucking that bitch!" she yelled and tried to fucking stab me. I shoved her back on the bed and grabbed the fucking knife. I turned around, and this crazy ass girl jumped on my back.

"Ahmad, how could you! I've given up everything to fucking be with you," she cried out, breaking my fucking heart. She was punching the shit out of my head. She even bit the side of my neck hard as fuck.

"Ah, shit! Pia, calm down," I yelled, not wanting to hurt her but just get her ass off of me. That stupid ass hoe Rowan put the fucking condom wrappers in my damn pocket. I swear when I saw that hoe it was going down.

"Pia," I grabbed her and tossed her onto the bed. She kicked the shit out of my leg before I jumped on top of her. I held both of her wrists down with one hand while I looked down at her writhe beneath me. This was the last thing I ever wanted to happen.

"I'm sorry. I fucked up ma," I said looking down at her. Her eyes filled with tears as she cried. With every tear that fell down her face, I felt even more fucked up. Fucking Rowan was not worth the pain I was putting her through. I knew I had to save face and fix this shit immediately.

"Pia, I'm sorry. I let her suck my dick, but that was it. No sex, I swear," I lied and kissed her neck. She moved at first until I stuck my tongue in her ear.

"I'm sorry…please forgive me. Please," I begged and kissed her sweet lips. She closed her eyes still crying. I let go of her wrists and took off her shirt then her bra. Her small breasts bounced as I slid down her body and took off her jeans along with her underwear. I kissed my way back up between her legs and slowly started to lay kisses on that pretty pussy of hers. Pia gave the sweetest fucking moan my ears had ever heard. My dick bricked instantly.

"Ahmad…we should wait," she said grabbing my head. I nodded and pulled her clit between my lips. Her protests immediately died out. She closed her eyes, and I filled her with two of my fingers while I sucked on her. Pia came quick as hell and soon I was taking off my shorts and sliding up her body. No condom because this was my pussy. I grabbed my mans and slowly slid him into her sweet spot. When I say I heard fucking angels singing, I'm not joking. Pia grabbed my arms and clenched her eyes shut. I'd busted Rowan's cherry, but it didn't feel shit like this. Maybe her ass was lying or some shit.

"Ahmad, slow down, please," she begged. I nodded and bent down to kiss her.

"You feel so fucking good P. I been waiting on this baby. I'mma make this pussy cum so good," I promised her and started to hit her with some slow deep strokes. I was blessed thank God with a lengthy little nigga, so Pia was struggling to take him at first. I had to push him all of the way in making her scream out in pain.

"Wait!" she yelled. I kissed her cheek then slid my tongue into her ear. That was her spot and always made her super wet. She moaned and started to slowly wind them hips.

"Yeah, ma. Move like you do when you in class. Fuck me back Pia, take your dick,"' I told her. She took my words to heart and started meeting me thrust for thrust. I closed my eyes and held my breath. I wanted to cum. I could feel it. Pia was too tight; the pussy was too wet, and this shit was all mine. It was too much for a nigga to bare.

"Damn, P I'm cumming," I said and pumped faster so that she could cum with me.

"Ahmad……baaabbbyyy," she moaned cumming at the same time that I did. I fell on top of her and pulled out when I was sure all of my seeds had filled her up. She was having my fucking baby.

*****

Run up them bands on the regular
Hitting my plug on the celly, yeah
Tell my ex-bitch that I'm sorry

"I'mma skate off in a Rari!" my uncle Kasam yelled with a bottle of Dom in his hands. I

nodded my head and blew weed smoke out of my mouth. My pops had surprised me with a little bachelor party and shit. I was good though because I knew my moms had taken Pia to the MGM so they could have a girl's spa night. I just prayed my aunties didn't clown on Portia's fraud ass. She didn't have a filter, and my aunts weren't to be fucked with. My auntie, Olivia would straight take that bitch out.

"*Cut it, cut it! Them bricks is way too high you need to cut it!*" My uncle Kadar rapped with his hand on this fine, dark-skinned chick's ass. Man, my mom's would kill us all if she knew they had me in KOD but I loved the fuck out of my pops for this.

"*Them prices way too high you need to cut it,*" I rapped along, tossing money to some broads bouncing that ass. My uncle, Aamil smirked at me.

"I ain't cutting shit," he joked, and we all laughed. I tried to get my nigga, Shyy to come, but his ass was sick as fuck. He may not have a chance to make my wedding and shit that was being held at the MGM hotel in one of their grand ballrooms.

"This is it, nigga. No more hoes, no more freedom. You might as well give Pia your balls the minute you say I do," my uncle, Kasam said smiling at me. I chuckled, but that shit wasn't happening. I was cutting Rowan off, but at the end of the day, I was still gonna be the fucking man in the relationship. She wasn't controlling my every fucking move, and this nigga was one to talk.

"Yeah, this coming from the nigga that takes his wife with him on tour and shit. You scared auntie gone roll up on you and shut some shit down," I said getting his ass back. He laughed because he knew that shit was true. My auntie didn't play. It was all over the internet about how she used to beat bitches down for coming at him. She has calmed down a lot now, but I knew that shit was still inside of her just waiting to get out.

Kasam sat back and blew some hookah smoke out of his mouth. That nigga looked just like me and my pops.

"Nah, at first I was on some fuck shit, but then I almost lost her. No matter how fat an ass is or how freaky a bitch gone be, she will never replace Erin. Only a fool would lose something irreplaceable for something that everybody done had. These hoes for everybody but, Erin, I know that she got my back. I know if I call her right now and be like bae I killed that nigga, she would be like come on let's bury the body. If I go broke, she grinding with me to get my money up. If I get sick, she nurturing a nigga back to health. Erin is my fucking rock. She holds together my household, and I'm quick to cut some shit short to run back home to her ass because she is something I can't lose. Nah, I'd fucking lose millions before I lose her. None of that shit gone matter anyway if she gone," he said dropping some real fucking knowledge on me. I couldn't do shit but respect that. I was scared as hell when Pia found that fucking condom. I never wanna feel like that again.

"I feel you, Unk. Auntie the truth. She be schooling Pia already on what to do and shit. Maybe that's why Pia pulled a fucking knife out on me the other night."

"She what?" My pops asked pushing this yellow-bone cutie out of his face. She had been on him hard all night. She must not know moms would wreck him and her ass at the same damn time in this bitch.

"No dance," she asked my pops and pushed her thongs to the side so that he could get a peek of her shaven kitty. It was fat and pretty no lie, but still this hoe was trying it.

"Nah, I'm good sweetie," my pops said with his hands on his head. She ignored him and bounced her ass on his lap, making sure to grind all slow on him and shit.

"Nah, bitch he said move," I said looking at her. My uncles laughed as she stood and

walked off rolling her beady ass eyes.

"Ahmad said bitch you ain't taking my momma spot," my uncle Kasam joked, but shit

that's how I felt. I ain't playing that shit, and if pops were to ever cheat on moms, I'd fuck that nigga up my damn self.

"Man, for real, though. Bitch needed to move around. She doing too much. I was about to call my momma," I said frowning. They all laughed at me, including my pops.

"Sophie got your ass trained good and shit," he said, smiling proudly at me.

"But, nah, Rowan put a damn condom wrapper in my pocket and while Pia was cleaning my room, she found it. Why did she put that shit in my food and then pull a fucking knife out on me? It was like she was fucking possessed or some shit. She ain't never acted like that before," I said shaking my head. I had to hit the blunt to shake that crazy ass vision out of my head.

"Shit, maybe she has then. If she would have been talking to your auntie Drew's ass she would have stabbed you with that bitch," my uncle Aamil said laughing.

"Nigga, if she would have been talking to Olivia she would have stabbed you in the shower with that shit, and you would have never seen it coming," my uncle Kadar laughed but was serious as hell. My auntie "O" was down like that. I chuckled. They all had some crazy ass wives. I didn't want Pia to be on that shit.

"I don't want no crazy ass wife, though," I said looking at all of them. My pops smiled.

"Then don't do shit for her to flip out on you for. Love makes women do crazy shit. As long as you don't play with her emotions, then she'll be good to you. Keep fuckin' around with Rowan and you gone make Pia do a 187 on both of y'all. She looks like she got it in her," he said, and I laughed because I knew for a fact that she did. She whipped that knife out on my black ass quick as fuck.

"Hell, yeah, she does but I'mma be a good ass husband, so that's not shit for me to worry

about," I said. They all gave me questioning looks, but they didn't call me out, and I respected them for that.

Chapter Thirteen

Pia

"Has Ameer ever cheated on you?"

Sophie stared at me. She was sipping wine wearing a black silk robe. We'd been getting pampered all day and the day had finally come to an end. Ahmad's aunts Drew and Erin had gotten drunk and were passed out in the other room while Portia rolled a joint at the table. His aunt Olivia and her sister Quinn sat on the other sofa talking to each other. Ahmad's great aunt was in a connecting room and his uncle Luke's wife was asleep in an adjoining room.

"Yes, he has. Even though he was still married to Ahmad's mother at the time, I was living with him. I don't want to go all into how it happened, but I found out the night he proposed that he had spent some time with her. I believe they had sex. To this day his black ass will deny it, but in my heart and mind I know the truth," she replied shocking the hell out of me.

"Wow," I said thinking about on how I found out Ahmad betrayed me. Sophie's chinky eyes stared at me intently.

"What did my son do?" she asked. Portia glanced over at us and a few seconds later she stood up. I groaned because

I did not want her in my business. She gave horrible advice. On top of that, she was dressed in a damn bra and thongs talking about she thought I was having a lingerie party. It was like she could never keep her fucking clothes on.

"Right, what did his cute little ass do this time?" she asked, sitting down. Sophie glanced over at her.

"Portia, this is Pia's night. Let's not ruin it," she said to her. Portia giggled and lit her joint.

"Sophie, please calm down. This is my daughter and my business," she said smiling. Sophie took a deep breath and sighed before turning back to me.

"Pia, please continue."

I glanced at Portia reluctantly before talking.

"I found out that Ahmad let Rowan give him oral sex. He apologized and said that it would never happen again. I believe him still I'm worried. She seems like she's always going to be in the background lurking looking for a chance to jump in my spot."

Portia laughed.

"Where is the hoe at? We can go handle that bitch right now," she said jumping up.

Olivia and Quinn walked over to the sofa and sat down next to me. Sophie shook her head. I could see that my news on Ahmad's cheating had hurt her. I wasn't trying to ruin the mood I just needed advice on what to do. How to prevent it from happening again.

"I'm sorry that happened. That reason alone makes me wish I had nothing but boys. Relationships aren't easy Pia, but you have to put your foot down early on and let him know that shit like that won't ever be tolerated. Cute or not, first love or not. You won't accept it," Sophie said to me and Quinn nodded with her in agreement.

Portia sat back down and looked my way.

"Look, baby, it's good you experienced this now. All men cheat. All of these bitches in here have been cheated on including me. Sophie is feeding you some bullshit, at the end of the day, Ahmad is young and rich. Shit, his daddy, is rich and has probably cheated on Sophie more times than she can fucking count. Don't lose your man listening to them. He's going to fuck up and probably will for at least ten to fifteen more years. But while he's doing him you can go out and do…"

"Bitch! Can you just stop it for one got damn minute," Olivia said snatching Portia up by her arm. It almost looked as if she was levitating the way Olivia dragged her out of the room. Quinn stood up and rushed after her while Sophie dropped her head. I knew it wasn't right, but couldn't help but to laugh. Damn, I'd wanted to snatch Portia for the longest.

"No "O"! Put her down. Let her neck go!" We heard Quinn yell.

"Nah, this bitch got it coming!" Olivia yelled back.

Sophie jumped up and went after them. They all came back ten minutes later, and Portia was smoking her joint with a shaky finger. I noticed a few of her tracks had come out, and she had a bruised lip. Olivia walked over hugging me from behind.

"I'm sorry for acting that way, Pia. Please forgive me. I need some help with my temper baby girl," she said and kissed my cheek. I nodded, and she walked back out the room refusing to look Portia's way. Portia rolled her eyes but didn't say shit which was for the best. Sophie sat back down beside me, and she touched my arm.

"Love is a lot of things, but it should never hurt Pia. With anyone you have to set boundaries. Especially with men. Ahmad is young, but that's no excuse. He is marrying you, and you're about to have his child. He either has to get his shit together or watch you be happy without him. Never allow for anyone to hurt you and be okay with it, Pia," she said. I nodded and rested my head on her shoulder.

"Thanks, Ma," I whispered and closed my eyes while she hummed one of Sade's songs.

*****

"Never knew I could love someone the way that I love you. You are my best friend, and I'm so ready to spend the rest of my life with you." My words got a little caught in my throat as I stared at Ahmad. I touched his face as my eyes watered. "I love you with my whole heart. You were put here for me and I for you. As long as you continue to breathe

I'mma hold you down because I know that you're going to do the same for me," I said to him. They say dreams do come true and at this exact moment, I believed it. Ahmad was standing in front of me in a black tux looking finer than anything I had ever seen before. He had a fresh ass caesar with a superb lineup. I creamed my panties just from staring at him. I loved everything about him from his thick brows down to his light skin that had some freckles here and there splattered across his face. Even down to his full luscious lips and almond shaped eyes. He was the shit and thankfully all mine.

I was wearing my white Vera Wang mermaid gown that fit me like a glove. I had a platinum diamond encrusted tiara on my head, and my makeup was done up, making me look older and feel so beautiful. We had no bridesmaids or groomsmen. It was just us, and I liked it like that because he was all that I needed.

"Pia," Ahmad stopped talking for a moment to clear his throat. Who knew cocky smart mouth ass Ahmad would ever be at a loss for words?

"Pia, that was beautiful bae. I'm not that fancy with my shit," he said, and Sophie gave him a look that made everyone laugh. He winked at her. "I'm not romantic like you so I'mma keep it simple. I belong to you, and you belong to me. That's it," he said, and I bit down hard on my bottom lip as my eyes watered. Ahmad grabbed my face and leaned down so that our foreheads could touch. "But, I do need you to give me a new promise," he said. My heart swelled at his words.

"What's that?" I whispered against his lips. He gazed into my eyes with those sexy eyes of his.

"I need for you to promise to always love me and to never let me go. Not even when you feel like that might be the easiest thing to do. I need for you to always believe in me and have my back because I'mma always ride for you. Can you promise to do that?" he asked in a tone only I could hear. I nodded immediately, and he smiled. He pecked my lips before pulling back.

Ahmad's pastor finished the rest of the ceremony and before I could blink Ahmad was pulling me into his arms. I cried tears of joy as he kissed me.

"My baby," I could hear Sophie cry. I kissed Ahmad, and we walked down the aisle. We went into the hallway to take pictures with both of our families, and I was able to change into a Tracy Reese dress while everyone went to the dining hall to eat. As Ahmad and I walked out the spotlight was on us.

"Now introducing Mr. And Mrs. Ahmad Matin," the DJ said, and everyone clapped and whistled. I clutched Ahmad's hand as tightly as I possibly could. I still couldn't believe this was happening. I was his wife. I was Ahmad's freaking wife! I was so happy I could scream.

"Play some music!" Kasam yelled, and everyone in the room with the exception of the older people flooded the dance floor.

You made me happy
This you can bet
You stood right beside me, yeah
And I won't forget
And I really love you

"You should know!" Ahmad sang hugging me from the back. "I wanna make sure I'm right, girl before I let go," he sang while I blushed. I bent over a little and pushed my ass against him. He chuckled.

"Get it neph!" Kadar yelled out, and everyone formed a circle around us. The DJ started playing Migos' *Look at Me Dab* and Ahmad, and my ignorant side came out.

Look at my dab, bitch dab
Look at my dab, bitch dab
Get in there, get in there
Get in there, get in there, bitch dab
Get in there, get in there, bitch dab

My baby was killing the dab until Kasam walked up and started dabbing with a damn bottle of D'usse in his hand.

"Get that nigga, Ahmad!" Ameer yelled while laughing.

Ahmad started milly rocking, and Kasam stopped dancing. My baby wasn't nothing nice on the dance floor.

"Get it, baby," I said doing the milly myself. Ahmad and I both loved to dance only he would do the ones that was nigga approved.

"I'mma let you have it since it's your day and shit otherwise I would embarrass your little ass out here," Kasam said wiping the sweat off of his forehead. I laughed and glanced around for my family. The only people I saw in the reception room was Portia. All of my family from out of town who had been at the wedding were gone, including my dad who thankfully showed up in enough time to walk me down the aisle and take pictures with me. I walked off of the dance floor and over to Portia, who was entertaining one of Ameer's business associates.

"Hey, where is everyone?' I asked her and looked around again. She put some Percocet in her mouth and smiled sexily at the man before responding to me.

"They left. Pia, you're one of them now so you can kiss your dad's family goodbye. They want nothing else to do with you. You've disgraced them, but oh well. They didn't like me, either. Fuck them," she said and laughed while walking off with the sexy dark-skinned guy. I felt like the walls were closing in on me as I quickly walked out of the ballroom. I fell down against the wall, and Ahmad rushed after me. My heart pounded inside of my chest at Portia's words.

Pia, you're one of them now so you can kiss your dad's family goodbye.

"Oh God," I cried out as he sat down beside me. He grabbed my face and forced me to look at him.

"What's wrong, ma?" he asked looking concerned. I shook my head, making my tears hit the top of my dress.

"They left. My dad, my Abuela, my family, are gone. They left me," I said quietly. All my life it had always been my dad, my brothers and me. I couldn't believe they would leave on a day that was so important to me. In my dad's country, people got married young all of the time, so I had a feeling they were more pissed at Ahmad being black over everything else. Which was bullshit because my dad and brothers dealt with more black women than any other race, yet I couldn't be with a black man and it be acceptable to them.

"Come here," he said pulling me into his arms. He kissed the top of my head, and I cried on him. I had never in my life felt so alone. I loved my dad and my family with all of my heart. I didn't wanna have to choose them over my husband, and if they really loved me, they wouldn't make me.

"I'm here, and I'mma always be here for you, Pia. I know it hurts, and I hate your pops did that hoe ass shit, but you got my family and me. We love you and you one of us now so everything will be okay baby," he promised me.

"Lick it," Ahmad said holding his long thick dick in my face. In my head, all I could think of was the video I had seen of Portia giving head. Some nights, it haunted my dreams. I tried my best to hold in my frown as I slowly licked him. He grabbed my head and forced himself into my mouth. With every thrust of his hips, I could hear him groan all animalistic and shit. I felt so degraded and disgusted by the act.

"Ugh, no! Stop, Ahmad!" I yelled, pulling back. He sighed with frustration. I felt bad, but sucking him off was something I just wasn't ready to do.

"Come here, Pia," he said sitting up in the king sized bed. I slowly got up and crawled over to him. I straddled him in nothing but my birthday suit, and he rubbed my ass.

"In bed, it's just us. No Portia, nobody else. I'm your husband, and you have to please me. I like getting my dick sucked and as my wife, you should wanna like that, too. Don't you like it when I'm licking on that pretty ass pussy of yours?" he asked. I nodded while staring at him.

"Yeah, you know I do."

"Then why wouldn't I like shit like that? We gotta work on that, ma," he said and slowly lifting me. He was hard, and I was wet and ready for him. Slowly I slid down him, and he slapped my ass. Sucking dick, I couldn't do, but riding was something I was falling in love with. It was just like dancing, and I loved to dance.

"Fuck me," he said staring into my eyes. I nodded and moved my hips slowly up and down on his dick.

"Oh…mmm," I moaned feeling him deep inside of me. I tried to close my eyes, and he pinched my nipple.

"Keep them open. I want you to look me in the eyes when you cum," he said making my body shake at his words.

"Okay," I said in a breathy tone. My hair was sweated the fuck out. My thigh was even cramping up on me, but I didn't stop. For him, I couldn't. I moved faster with sweat rolling down the center of my chest. He leaned in and licked it up. He grabbed my hips and forced me to move faster. Ahmad was always taking control, even when I was on top. I guess there was no topping a man like him.

"Stop playing and fuck me, Pia. Make this dick bust all inside that pussy," he commanded and had me fucking him so hard I couldn't reply. My legs were like rubber, yet I didn't complain. My head fell back, and my body fell into him. With my face buried into his neck, I exploded onto his dick. It was the greatest feeling I had ever experienced. A few minutes later he came deep inside of me. We both fell onto the bed on our backs. Ahmad rolled over onto me and kissed my lips. I was good for a nap, but I saw he was ready for round two.

"Ain't no sleeping. This our wedding night. We gotta make a baby," he said and before I could respond he was back inside of me. My legs were pulled up on to his shoulder, and I had my hand on his damn abs that were outlined so perfectly you would think they were drawn on. He slapped my hands away smiling.

"Stop that shit. You can take it," he said like he was a little nigga. I was pissed until he started hitting my spot. My leg twitched, and he grinned.

"See. Daddy hitting that spot, huh? My pussy like that?" he asked and hit it again. I nodded feeling my orgasm vastly approaching.

"You know I do baby," I moaned.

Ahmad smirked.

"Yeah, I do. Suck on this," he said and stuck his pretty tongue out of his mouth while leaning down. I pulled his tongue between my lips, and he went to town on my shit. Making me quickly release all over him.

"Have my baby," he said sliding in and out of me still so damn hard. I moaned. Damn. Did he really think I could say no with him inside of me like this?

"I wanna…. please let me have your baby," I begged ready to ask him for anything at the damn moment. He smiled, and I could see pure satisfaction on his face.

"I'mma fill this pussy up with cum. You gonna have all of my babies Pia," he said. His hips moved at a feverish pace as he fucked me unmercifully and soon his cum was once again deep inside of me.

Chapter Fourteen

Pia

Over the next month, I transitioned from living with my dad to living with Ahmad and his family. Sophie had given us the whole guest house which was big as hell. She'd even had it cleaned out, so I was free to decorate it however I liked. We were a month away from prom, and I was two days away from going to the doctor which meant it was time to come clean. Ahmad had been spending a lot of time getting ready for college basketball, so I was left to chill with either his family or by myself.

My dad had drained my bank account and rarely took my calls. I wasn't even sure if he was going to see me off to prom or come to my graduation. Portia had moved here to be with Ameer's business associate and was talking about marrying him. He had a daughter that was a year older than me. She seemed like a cool chick, so I had plans on hooking up with her in the near future. I didn't think in a million years I would be without my dad, and it was something I wasn't willing to accept just yet.

"Here take this," Ahmad said dropping three boxes of pregnancy tests onto my lap. He kissed my cheek and walked off. "I gotta go to the school, Pia. Ma said can you keep the girls for a little while later on," he said before leaving the bedroom. I sighed as my phone buzzed on the bed. I picked it and looked at the screen.

Xerius: *what's up Pia? You coming to my birthday dinner girl??? Please…*

"Pia, take the test real quick before I go!" Ahmad yelled from the other room.

I wasn't trying to have a baby, but I had been negligent in using condoms, and I wasn't on birth control. Every time I mentioned going to get on something, Ahmad started bugging out talking all crazy and shit. It got to the point where I just gave up, but I will say that every time he came I said a little prayer, hoping a baby wasn't made. I wasn't ready for kids, and I knew that if I wasn't carrying his child, I was coming clean about the lie and taking my ass down to the nearest clinic to get on something immediately. Whether he liked the shit or not.

I put my phone away and went to the connecting bathroom to take the test. Ahmad walked into the bathroom with my phone in his hands a few minutes after I did. I already knew what he was looking at so I chose not to say anything. It was too early in the morning to be arguing with him over nothing. I hated how Ahmad felt like he had the right to go through my shit when he had his phone on FBI lockdown and shit.

"When I see this fuck nigga it's over for him. I blocked his shit, and if I catch you talking to him again I'm fucking you up Pia, now what does it say?" he asked setting my phone down on the sink. I stared at him angrily. Who the fuck did he think he was? My husband or my daddy?

"Ahmad, don't go through my phone. I don't do that to you so show me the same respect. Xerius is just a friend that I had before we were married and I wasn't going to his dinner."

Ahmad looked at me. He was rocking some black jogging pants that were sagging off of his narrow waist, with a black beater that had his muscular arms on display. Ahmad had a good amount of tattoos covering his body but of course, my favorite was the one on his hand. His caesar was perfectly lined up along with his beard like the ones his dad and uncles had, and it looked sexy as fuck on him. In just the short amount of time we'd been together, he looked older and more mature. His hazel eyes were staring at me angrily as if he wanted to take my head off. I handed him the test and wiped myself before flushing the toilet.

"Yeah, okay," he said tossing the test into the trash.

"I'll tell them you lost it. Play sick and I'll be able to come home early today and chill with you," he said and walked out of the bathroom. I took another test and almost immediately the lines came back positive. I couldn't believe my eyes. I took another test out of the box and had the same results. I was so nervous my damn hands started to shake.

"Pia…oh my God," I said looking at all of the tests I had taken. I finished handling my business in the bathroom and wrapped all of the tests in some tissue paper. I grabbed some money out of Ahmad's stash that his dad was giving us, and I exited the bedroom. I slide my feet into my espadrilles and left the house. Sophie was letting me use her old Mercedes since my dad had taken my car. I got in and headed straight to the closest clinic I could find. I sat with the positive pregnancy tests in the passenger's seat wrapped in a black plastic bag. I closed my eyes and said a quick prayer. I was scared, but the thought of being a mother at only seventeen was something I wasn't ready for. I had to do this then I would get on birth control. A few years from now Ahmad and I could try and have a baby. Once we were both in better positions in life.

"God please forgive me for this. If they say I am indeed pregnant, then I will have no choice but to get rid of it. God, please judge my mind and not my heart. I'm just not ready," I said and exited the car with my plastic bag in tow. I tossed it into the trashcan by the front door of the clinic. After signing in and taking care of the paperwork, I sat down.

I looked around and saw all of these young and older women in the waiting area looking to get rid of their child. I believed no one could tell a woman what to do with her body, so I didn't judge them however I wasn't trying to make this a damn habit. I was seen an hour later, and I tested positive again for being pregnant. I paid for the abortion bill and took it. The nurse instructed for me to go straight home and call 911 if I experienced any extreme pain.

I rode home in silence with small cramps filling my stomach and back. I had purchased some big maxi pads from the drugstore and had even made a follow-up appointment to get on birth control in a few weeks. I had so much on my mind and was looking to vent. I arrived at the house, and I spotted Sophie standing outside of the house with wet eyes. She saw me and started walking my way before I could even get out of the car. I got out, and she immediately pulled me into her arms.

"I'm so sorry, baby. You shouldn't be driving," she said hugging me tightly.

"I had to get some pads," I said feeling my own eyes water. She was crying about a child I had miscarried, and I was about to cry for the child I was killing with a pill. We were both very emotional.

"Ahmad could have done that," she said grabbing the bag from me. Sophie followed me back to the guest house and helped me get into bed. She made me some soup and even cleaned the room which was mostly Ahmad's stuff. He had more clothes than he knew what to do with them. He'd only brought over 10% of his clothes from the house and still he couldn't fit them all into the closet with my clothes. Sophie sat with me for the rest of the day, and once Ahmad came home, I was bleeding extremely heavy. He looked at me as I walked out of the bathroom with my period panties on and I broke down. I wanted to tell him the truth. I swear I did. However, I knew that telling him about what I did would cause issues with us when we had just got married. I knew he wouldn't understand how I felt. He had everything he ever wanted happening for him right now and while I was happy to have him I had lost my family in return. I couldn't lose the last little bit of independence I had. Being a parent was a sacrifice, and it was one I wasn't willing to make at the moment. I chose Pia, and I knew Ahmad would have hated me for it.

"Pia, come here," he said hugging me tightly. I broke down in his arms. I opened my mouth and did something I had never done before. I lied to him.

"Ahmad, I think I'm losing a baby for real. I have been bleeding bad all day," I said crying into his tank top. Ahmad's heartbeat quickened as Sophie and Ameer walked back into the room.

"Is she okay?" Ameer asked sounding really worried about me.

"Nah, she's bleeding bad. I'm going to help her lay back down. I just need a minute," he said, and I could hear him sniffle. I wasn't sure if he was crying or not because it was so quick. He took me back to the bed and propped me up to help with my bleeding. Then he left the room with his dad behind him. Sophie came over to the bed and sat down. Even a crying mess she still looked insanely beautiful. She moved some of my hair out of my face and kissed my cheek.

"I know I was upset with you two, but I never wanted for this to happen. I wanted to meet my first grandbaby," she said with a tear rolling down her cheek. I closed my eyes to hold my tears. Me not taking that pill could have avoided all of this pain. Guilt was slowly invading my body.

"I know, Ma. I know," I whispered.

"Where is she! Pia!" Portia yelled frantically running into the room. I opened my eyes and looked at her. She actually looked hurt and concerned for me. She rushed over to me and kissed my face. Sophie stood and wiped her eyes again.

"I'll give you two some privacy," she said, and I'm sure it was so that she didn't argue with Portia at a time like this. Portia sat down and grabbed my hand. She looked down into my eyes and her eyes watered. I had never seen her so distraught.

"Pia, I have to know," she said rubbing my hand.

I frowned.

"Know what Portia?"

She took a deep breath and sighed.

"Did you sign a prenup?" she asked.

"Ahmad!" I yelled out with the last little bit of strength I had. Ahmad along with his mom and dad rushed back into the room. Sophie looked at Portia and shook her head.

"What did you do?" she asked her.

Portia let my hand go and licked her glossy lips.

"I was making sure she was okay. I know how you people are. I want to make sure my daughter will be straight. Because of your son she no longer has her inheritance and I don't get fucking child support from her father, so I asked her did she sign a prenup. That baby was our insurance policy," she said unapologetically. Sophie lunged at her.

"You, stupid bitch," she said as Ameer picked her up. He carried her out of the room as Ahmad walked over to the bed. He was unusually quiet and calm. He sat beside me and looked down into my eyes.

"Pia, do you trust me?" he asked with swollen eyes. I nodded. Of course, I did.

"Then I need for you tell your mom not to contact you for a while. She's toxic, bae. She only gives you negative energy and she is no longer welcome in my house," he said still looking down into my eyes. I felt a huge lump form in the middle of my throat. Yes, I trusted him, yes I loved him, but Portia was all I had left on my side of the family. Could I cut her off like that? Damn, she was selfish and ignorant as hell, but she was still the woman that had brought me into this world.

"Pia, this is only the beginning. Once you cut me off then starts the beating. Shit, he's already doing the cheating," she said. Ahmad's eyes widened, and he nodded his head. I knew he was getting pissed off at her.

"None of us are perfect Portia. You should know that better than anybody with your porn star ass," he said finally turning his eyes her way. Portia gasped.

"Pia, I'm your mother. I've given up my life in Chicago to be here for you," she lied through her perfect set of white teeth. I closed my eyes and hummed through my cramps. I was dealing with too much at one time.

"Pia, it's her or me. This bitch doesn't give a fuck about you and you know it. I'mma always have your back baby, but this hoe has to go," he said getting off of the bed.

"Ahmad, chill out that's still her mom," his dad said from across the room. Portia stood and kissed my cheek. I opened my eyes and looked at her. I couldn't believe all of this bullshit was happening to me.

"It's okay sweetie. I know I'm not perfect. I've made a lot of mistakes, but I am who I am Pia. I'm your mother, and I might have a fucked up way of showing it, but I do love you with all of my heart. I don't want to cause you any more pain. I'll go, and when things are good again, you can call me. I'm marrying Tremaine and were going to start a family together. I only want you to be happy…that's the least I could do," she said with tears streaming down her face. I had never in my life seen her so emotional. She dropped her head and walked out of the room. Ameer followed after her as Ahmad looked my way. He walked over to the bed and sat down. I expected for him to hold me or even caress my aching stomach but got neither. He laid back on the pillows and went to sleep. A man that I loved so much and had given up so much to be with was making me slowly feel something for him that I never knew that I could. *Hate.*

Chapter Fifteen

Ahmad

I sat across from the woman that birthed my biological moms Tatum in silence. This shit was wild, and I wasn't sure how to feel about it at the moment. So far she had been showing me pictures of her, and that was cool considering my pops didn't have any pictures of her besides the one from their wedding that he had given me already. I noticed how much I looked like her and shit, and I felt a little sad. From what I could remember she was always gone, but maybe we had good times too, and I just forgot about them. Maybe she was a good ass mom to me but then if that was the case why would my pops lie to me? That nigga has always kept it one hundred with me whether I liked the shit or not.

"These were her brothers Trent and Tahj. They were killed as well by…*your father*," she said, and I arched my brow. I knew that, and my pops had broken the real story down to me on how they kidnapped my auntie Erin and shit trying to get at him. They deserved that plus more, but for her to say as well like he had something to do with my mom's dying had me hot.

"But what you mean by as well? Floyd's enemies had them, and Tatum killed," I asserted correcting her. She looked at me through her rectangular Gucci eyeglasses and sighed. She was in her sixties and holding up pretty good for herself. She looked like an older version of Tatum.

"Baby, your daddy killed your momma because she didn't wanna be with him. That's a fact, and if he weren't so rich, I would have been able to build a case against him. He took all of my kids away from me," she said blinking away her tears. "I'm afraid of him, so I beg of you to keep this conversation between us, but I know he killed her, and that damn Luke guy helped. He was the one that tossed her out onto the streets when she left your father. He wouldn't even let her take any clothes with her," she said while shaking her head. I stared at her. She was making this sound like a horror story, but these were my people she was talking about. The same people that she claimed killed my mom and all they had ever done was love and take care of me. I couldn't believe they would ever do some snake shit like that no matter what Tatum did off the fact that she was my moms. If anything my pops would have just let her go and cut her off. I couldn't even vision him killing her and wrapping her in a blanket like some gutter trash. Nah, my pops would never do no shit like that.

"I won't tell him anything."

"If you do that's cool too. It's a new day, and if your pops want it, then it's whatever," this light skinned nigga said stepping into the room that resembled me a little too much.

"Boy, calm down. This is your first cousin, Ahmad. Ahmad, this is Trent's son Tucker but we I call him Tuck," she said smiling at the last part. I guess he hated that lame ass name he had and shit. I stood up and grilled this nigga because I didn't appreciate that hot shit he was saying about my pops. Tuck stared at me for a moment before laughing. I could tell that nigga didn't give a fuck just like me.

"Get you old pretty ass over here boy," he said pulling me into a hug.

"Mother Tuck!" my granny yelled, and we both laughed.

"Let's go blow one nigga," Tuck said in a lower tone grinning at me. Yeah, my family on my pops side resembled me, but this nigga here. Shit he damn near looked like he could be my brother and shit. I smiled. No lie it felt good to be around him. A big part of me always wondered what this side of my family was like. I just hated saying that to my pops because it always put him in a sour ass mood.

"Hell, yeah let's go," I said chuckling. My granny stood and walked over to me. She had a few tears falling from her eyes, and I felt bad to see her in distress. I hugged her small frame as she rubbed my back.

"You boys are all I have left in this world besides my sister Lucille. Please, Ahmad, don't close us out of your life. Our blood is running through you too, and your mom really loved you. Let me go get this recording I had of when you were a baby," she said and walked away. She came back into the room a few minutes later with this old ass digital camera. She handed it to me along with a charger.

"I'll have more pics and videos when you come back to see me. Don't forget about your granny, Ahmad," she said smiling at me. I smiled and kissed her cheek. As long as they were keeping it real with me, I would fuck with them.

"Now you know I can't do that granny," I said, and she laughed. She looked so happy just to be around me. That shit made me feel good as hell.

"Alright g-ma we out," Tuck said leading the way. We walked out of my granny's spacious Rosedale Park home and went out to the backyard. She had this big ass gazebo and deck. Her shit was laid, and I was happy to see she was doing well for herself. It didn't compare to my pops or people's shit, but granny was living nicely.

"Man, it's crazy that you here right now. We thought we would never get to fuck with you like that," Tuck said breaking down a big sack of weed onto the table. I sat back, and my phone vibrated in my pocket. I pulled it out and saw it was my baby calling. After Pia lost our baby for real shit had been strained with us. I knew she was mad at me telling her mom to stay away, but it was for the best. Portia had her all fucked up in the head and the sooner she got out of our lives the better my baby would be and our relationship. Coming in there talking about some fucking money. Pia was married to me so she would be okay regardless. Fuck what that bitch was talking about.

"What's up, ma," I said, taking the call before she hung up.

Pia sighed on the other end of the phone. She must have been pissed about something.

"You were supposed to watch Soraya tonight. I been studying for a test and I'm tired Ahmad," she complained. That damn whine of hers was starting to irritate the fuck out of a nigga.

"Ma, I had some really important shit to do. Just have the kids sit out in the living room by the tv while you rest."

"Okay, like Ameerah is gonna do that. Whatever Ahmad," she said and ended the call. I put my phone away, and my cousin was staring at me.

"Nigga, you got kids?" he asked with wide eyes. I shook my head shit I almost did.

"Nah, that's my wife. She watching my sisters for me. Mad that I'm not at home and shit."

Tuck sat with a smirk on his face.

"Wife, hold on. How old are you again?" he asked.

I laughed.

"Nigga, I'm seventeen, but yeah I just got married and shit. My wife was about to have to leave the country, so I did what I had to do," I replied.

My cousin gave me this silly ass grin.

"Something foreign huh?' he asked. I hated that type of slave, nigga mentality shit. I wasn't one of those niggas that just had to have a mixed chick on his arm. I didn't give a fuck what race Pia was. Shit, I had fallen in love with her way before she grew into her looks any fucking way.

"She's Mexican and Puerto Rican, but she looks just like us…some niggas," I said being truthful. Pia was light as hell but off the top, you would just think she was a light-skinned black female. Still, that type of shit didn't matter to me. I loved Pia for the down ass chick she was. She could be black as coal, and I would still love her old ugly ass.

"She's my baby, though. Fuck looks when it comes down to it we all mixed with some shit," I said dropping the subject of Pia. I didn't like to have nobody up in my mix like that especially some nigga I had just met family or not.

"So you still in school and shit?" Tuck asked lighting the blunt.

"Yeah, I'm'a about to go to college in a few months to play ball and shit."

He smiled at me proudly.

"That's what's up. Granny watched some of your games on ESPN. She was always bragging on you and shit. I'mma street nigga, but I'm glad to see you were able to break the chain. That generational curse shit ain't no hoe. We breaded from hustlers, so the shit is just in us," he said and puffed on the blunt. I nodded. It was hard to stay on the straight and narrow, but not as hard as people would have thought. My pops didn't show me none of his street life shit, so I don't feel like I'm missing out on shit. Every now and then I get curious, but I know my pops and uncles would fuck me up if I even considered selling drugs. They'd bury my ass before I even hit the block.

"Man, my pops would kill me if I went to the streets. I've been to private schools my whole life and shit," I said chuckling. Tuck smirked at me.

"Shit, I was raised in the trap. When my pops got killed, his right hand took over and put me on when I was sixteen. I've been doing that shit ever since then. I'm proud of you, though. I'm glad to see one of us make it," he said. I nodded, and he cleared his throat. "I mean a nigga living well no doubt, but it's gotta feel good to be able to live a life where you not watching your fucking back all of the time. I'm not trying to do this shit forever. Just a few more years," he said looking off. I stayed quiet. Shit, that's what every hustler said, and either ended up getting locked up or killed. My peoples lucked out. Still, it came with casualties. My uncle, Aamil had to do some time, and my uncle Kasam damn near lost his life.

"So what, is this shit with my pops over? I can't be fucking with you and you feeling some type of way about my family and shit," I told him.

He passed me the blunt.

"It's over. As long as they cool with you being around us, then we are too. I'm just trying to live a long life while getting money. That's it," he replied. I blew smoke out of my mouth and smiled.

"Exactly."

*****

Hours later, I walked into the house blown out of my fucking mind. Tuck had taken me to the strip club and after drinking and watching them, sexy ass dancers bounce their ass I was on one. My dick was hard as a missile as I walked into the guest house in search of my bae. I found her asleep on the couch with her reading glasses still on. I smiled. She was the sexiest thing in the fucking world to me. She had on a t-shirt, and it had risen over her ass. I took her glasses off, and she didn't budge. I went down to the end of the couch and gently started to kiss on her creamy soft stomach. Her skin always smelled like shea butter. I opened her thighs and sniffed her panties. My pussy was calling me, and I was about to put a hurting on that shit.

"Ahmad…no," she whined, swatting my head away. I ignored her and grabbed the top of her panties. I pulled them down half way, and she jumped like she was on fire. Pia looked at me with the damn sleep still in her eyes and frowned.

"Ahmad, you stayed out all night while I watched your sisters, then you come home trying to fuck? I'm tired as hell. You should have thought about that shit before you chose to be a selfish ass nigga," she said scowling at me. She walked off, and I went after her. I took off my stuff and climbed into bed with her. I slid up behind her and put my arm around her slim waist.

"I'm sorry. I went to see my granny on my mom's side and ended up meeting my cousin. Time got away from me.

Let me make it up to you," I said and kissed her neck. She shook her head but that body…it was saying yes. Her skin was already warming up for a nigga. I pushed her back. I climbed on top of her and started kissing her on those soft ass lips of hers.

"I'm sorry baby, but I miss you…" I looked her in the eyes. The lights were off, but we could see each other because of the hallway light being on. "I miss my wife. She gotta come back to me. I mean you did promise a nigga you would always be there," I said making her smile. I always knew how to break down those fucking walls she was forever putting up.

"Let daddy in tonight," I said and pushed her thighs open with my legs. I was already naked and hard as fuck. I slowly rubbed my dick against her opening secreting the head with her juices. Pia moaned and arched her back off of the bed. We hadn't had sex since she'd lost the baby and I was so fucking horny it was crazy. Not calling Rowan was one of the hardest things I had to do, but I was trying to do right by Pia. I never wanted her to cry again because of a reckless decision I made.

"I'm about to fuck the shit out of you," I said and slowly slid inside of her. I lifted both of her legs into the crooks of my arms and deep stroked that pussy. Pia dug her long ass nails into the skin on my forearm.

"Ahmad! Shit! Baby!" she moaned while her pussy clenched me like a fist. I was high and drunk. There was no taking it easy on the pussy tonight.

"Shut that shit up, Pia," I said and hit it harder. Pia closed her eyes, and her mouth fell open. She was getting so wet you could hear me sliding in and out of her with every pump I made. I groaned and bit down hard on my bottom lip. I was trying not to bust before she did.

"This my pussy, Pia?"

Pia nodded, and I popped her in the mouth. Her eyes popped open, and she glared at me before that dick hit her spot so good it made her eyes roll into the back of her head.

"I said is this my pussy, Pia?" I asked with my balls tightening.

"Yessss!" she yelled, cumming all over my dick. I pulled out of her and rushed up her body. I tried to cum in her mouth, and she moved her head to the side. I ended up cumming all over the fucking pillow and in her hair. Before I could even cum all of the way, she was jumping out of the bed.

"You came in my fucking hair, Ahmad! What the fuck!" She yelled running out of the room. I fell back onto the bed trying to catch my breath. I closed my eyes and thought of Rowan and how she would guzzle my cum and swallow my dick whole. She was too trill for that shit. I smirked and eventually dozed off to sleep.

"I love this little boy. He's so freaking cute," Tatum said into the camera. I smiled with a huge ass lump in my throat. I saw how happy she and my pops were and for the first time in years I wished she was still alive. I wished they could have somehow made that shit work because then just maybe she would be here and not dead because of that bitch ass nigga she was with. I sighed and put the camera away. My body and mind were just tired. My life at the moment was all fucked up. I somehow found myself outside of Rowan's place. I knew it wasn't right. My mind was telling me the shit was wrong but my dick…. shit it was hard. Pia was whiny all of the fucking time and a damn headache. I still loved her no doubt, but she was getting on my fucking nerves. She was out getting fitted for her prom dress, and I was about to get my shit off. Hey, it is what it is.

"Hey you," Rowan said sliding into my car. I looked over at her, and my eyes skimmed over her outfit. She was wearing a black mini dress that fit her like a glove. I was instantly on hard from staring at her.

"Look, it's like this. The minute you step out of line we done and I promise you I'll never bless you with this dick again. Okay?" I said looking at her. Rowan eagerly nodded her head. She leaned over and pulled my shit out of my shorts. I was sweaty but to a freak like her, she gave no fucks. I reclined my seat, and she started doing some tricks with that tongue that had my fucking toes curling. I was thankful as hell for my tint.

"Shit girl," I said groaning. I grabbed her head, and she went all the way down. She even pulled my fucking balls into her mouth. The minute I felt the back of her throat I shot off my load.

"Fuck……damn……shit," I said and twitched in her mouth. Rowan sat with a satisfied smirk on her face. I pulled a condom out of the bag I had just gotten from the store and ripped it open. I gave it to her, and she put it on with her tongue. She climbed over to me and slowly sat down onto my dick. Rowan was tight. Her pussy felt nothing like Pia's, but I would be a lying nigga If I said it wasn't good.

"I missed you, baby," she said, and I covered her mouth with my hand. I began to beat that shit up from under her. I didn't want her thinking this was love. We were only fucking.

"Yes! Yes! Fuck me!" she yelled and slapped the shit out of me. She smiled and hit me again. No lie that shit made my dick harder. I grabbed her by her neck, and she started bouncing so hard on my dick we made my truck shake.

"Yeah ride this dick. You hear me bitch," I said, and she moaned.

"Mmmm, I hear you, daddy," she replied, and we both came at the same time.

Chapter Sixteen

Pia

"Oh my goodness," Sophie said as Ahmad and I took pictures together. On the outside, we looked so happy, but in reality, we were nothing like we used to be. Ahmad had been staying out late and doing all kind of sneaky shit. I was torn because for some reason I was mad at him, I just wasn't exactly sure why. I wanted him to console me more on the loss of the baby even though it was my fault I miscarried. I knew it was strange, but it was how I had been feeling.

"One more and you all can go," Erin said taking a few pictures of us. Ahmad and I both smiled playing the part. Ahmad was wearing a white tux, with a tan shirt, red tie, and white Christian Louboutin loafers. I was dressed in a nude long-sleeve lace dress that was form fitting at the top, with a deep v-cut and flowed out at the bottom and nude pumps. My hair was in a high layered bun. I loved the look I was working. It was sexy yet classy. Sophie and Ahmad's aunties had helped me pick it out. Sadly, I hadn't talked to Portia since the night I lost my baby. You never really know how much you miss someone until they leave your life. I missed my dad, my brothers and even her. Ahmad's family was cool, and I did love them but being around them daily made me think of my family that had seemed to forget about me.

"Look at nephew killing that suit! Gone be the freshest nigga in the building!" Kasam yelled snapping pictures of us on his phone. Ahmad released my hand and started posing. I moved to the side and watched him show out with a few of his boys that had come over to leave out with us. Sophie and Ameer took pics with him, and he rotated with all of his family while I watched. I scanned all of the people, hoping to see my dad, but I didn't. I cleared my throat and walked away with the end of my gown trailing behind me.

"Pia, are you okay?" Jess, Ahmad's cousin Mauri wife asked me. She looked gorgeous with her glowing skin and round belly. I smiled and gently rubbed her stomach.

"Yes, I'm good. A little tired," I lied. I was irritated as hell, but being with Ahmad lately, I had gotten used to being upset.

She looked me up and down.

"You know you could come work with me during the summer before you leave for school. I could always use some help since Isis retired," she replied. Jess ran a business that helped battered and abused women.

"Yeah, that would be nice," I said liking the idea of getting out of the house. I felt so alone at times. Jess smiled at me.

"Cool, then it's set. Just call me when you're ready," she said and walked away.

"Come on, Pia!" Ahmad yelled as everyone started to load into their cars. Ameer was letting Ahmad, and I take out his baby. His new matte gray Murcielago. I would say it was a beauty. Ahmad stared at it for a moment before he and I walked over to the hood. He looked deep into my eyes. I could see the Ahmad I had loved for so long. What hurt was that I felt like that person was fading away more and more.

"You look beautiful as hell today," he said, and I smiled at him. I touched his cheek, and they started snapping more pictures of us.

"Thanks, baby."

He smiled, licked his lips and leaned towards me. I closed my eyes as I kissed him and heard a bunch of "awe's" chorus around us.

"My babies," Sophie said as I pulled away from him. The way Ahmad's hazel eyes devoured me, I found myself getting a little wet. I bit down on my bottom lip, and he chuckled. He leaned towards me and pulled my bottom lip into his mouth.

"Alright now Ahmad," Sophie said making everyone laugh. He kissed me and pulled back.

"Ma, this my wife," he said, and it seemed to get eerily quiet outside. I saw a sexy ass dude that was a little taller than Ahmad appeared with a beautiful older woman. They hugged Ahmad while his family grilled them with questioning eyes.

"Pops, this is my cousin Tuck, and this is my granny. You know her. Granny that's my ma, Sophie, and my wife,

Pia," Ahmad said looking from his granny to his parents than me. While I quickly hugged his grandmother, Ameer stared at them. The look he gave Ahmad's grandma sent chills up and down my spine. Ahmad's grandmother pursed her lips and grabbed Tuck's hand. She seemed to lean into him for support. Tuck stood by smirking and looking so confident. I could tell him, and Ahmad had similar personalities. I instantly got a bad vibe off of him. It was as if he had a dark cloud following him around.

"What's up, Unk?" he asked smiling at Ameer. His tone was respectful, but I called bullshit on him.

"What up. Aye, Ahmad let holla at you," Ameer said looking so angry his light skin started to turn a darker shade. Ahmad grabbed my hand.

"Later Pops, or more like tomorrow. I gotta go. Thanks for coming Granny and Tuck. I'll holla at you, nigga," Ahmad said and pulled me away. Ahmad's cousin and granny quickly left while Ahmad and I got into the car. I looked at Sophie and could see she was trying to calm Ameer down while his uncles watched his cousin's every move until he pulled off in his truck. Ahmad drove off, and I glanced over at him.

"Your cousin seems off. Like he on some slick stuff," I said trying to say it in the best way that I could.

Ahmad frowned at me.

"What? You don't even fucking know him, Pia. That nigga is just like me, and he is cool as hell. My people are already about to be tripping. I would at least expect you to be on my fucking side since you my wife. Shit that's the least you could do," he said and cut the radio on.

The least I could do? I turned down the radio, and he pinched the shit out of my hand. He was so fucking childish.

"Pia, it's prom night. We about to have a good fucking time. If you wanna start talking shit I can take you back to the fucking house right now," he said and cut the music back up. I pulled my bottom lip into my mouth. I couldn't believe he was talking to me so reckless. Yeah, he was an asshole, but to me, he had always been a little sour and a lot of sweet. Sort of like a damn Sour Patch Kid. This nigga was straight sour and gave no fucks about how I felt about it. My phone vibrated in my hand, and I glanced down at it.

Xerius: *see you at the prom sweet p.*

I smiled. I quickly erased the message before Ahmad saw it and stared out of the window. Xerius went to the same private school that I attended so I had no clue who he was bringing to Ahmad's prom, but the fact that I would get to see him there was cool. I hadn't talked to him since Ahmad caught me texting him the last time because I didn't want to have any more drama in my life. All I hoped for was that if Ahmad did see him that he didn't show his ass. With Ahmad you never knew.

It took us fifteen minutes to get to Ahmad's school. He parked, and we got out. We walked with his friends and Ahmad was back in a good mood. He held my hand and even kissed my cheek a few times. I didn't have any friends from this school besides Zaria when we were cool, so I just waved at a few people I knew, but kept it moving. I guess if I hadn't been best friends with the most wanted nigga in the school I could have been more popular but who knows. I'm not much of a people person so my circle probably would have still remained small.

"Look at the Matins!" One of Ahmad's teammates yelled as we walked into the Country Club. He walked over to his friends, and they all started dapping each other up. I spotted Zaria walking in with this cutie that I used to have Geometry with. She looked at me and quickly turned her head. She looked good, and if it weren't for prom, I would have surely slapped her ass. I still haven't forgotten about the way she had me jumped. I was trying to keep it classy for the night, so I went back to Ahmad's side, and we all walked into the decorated ballroom.

Chapter Seventeen

Ahmad

After taking a few pictures with Pia, she went to talk to this one bitch she had a class with before she left and I dipped off with my niggas to blow back a few blunts. We leaned on the back of my pops Murcielago talking shit. I was feeling good and getting lifted. Pia was indeed shutting shit down, and I knew for sure we were the best-dressed couple here. I was pissed she couldn't get nominated for prom queen because she goes to a different school but that didn't matter. She was my queen every day of the week so fuck some high school ass title.

"There go your bitch," my nigga Shyy said tapping my leg. I looked up and watched Rowan's sexy ass get out of this old school Mercedes. She was wearing a strapless dress with this crystal looking shit all over it and a long ass train that some lame nigga was carrying for her. My dick bricked at the way she fitted that dress. No way would I have let Pia wear some shit like that, but Rowan was killing her fit. Every nigga in the parking lot was looking at her sexy ass body as she walked over to us. I blew a cloud of smoke as she approached me.

"Hey, zaddy," she purred. I nodded my head and looked at her lame nigga. This nigga was tall and gumpy, as hell. How the fuck he carrying a bitch dress for her and she get to walk over and call another nigga zaddy? I would have instantly dropped that shit and cursed her ass out. I guess these niggas would do whatever to sample some shit I could get on the regular.

"Ahmad, this is Jake. He's my date for the night. He was just accepted to Wayne State to play basketball," she said looking at me. I leaned in so only she could hear me loud and clear.

"Rowan, do I look like I give a fuck who this nigga is or what he does?" I asked making my niggas laugh. Rowan rolled her eyes, and her nigga mumbled something, but he didn't speak up, so I let his ass slide. I wouldn't be able to explain to Pia anyway why I fucked up Rowan's date.

"Make sure I get a dance," Rowan leaned towards me with this nigga still holding the back of her fucking dress. "And a ride on that long ass dick," she whispered to me before walking off swinging that plump ass of hers. Me and my niggas watched it move from side to side. I shook my head while willing myself to calm down. Rowan's ass was trouble.

"Nigga, don't look too hard. Pia gone fuck both of y'all up," one of my niggas said. I chuckled. Shit he was right about that.

"I know. I gotta watch Rowan's slick ass, let's roll out," I said and passed Shyy the blunt. To me, Pia was precious like a rare diamond. I always watched out for her even when she felt like I wasn't. I didn't want her in there with Rowan and Zaria because if anything was to happen to her, I was going to jail tonight. Some might call it petty, but I would slap a bitch that tries to hurt my bitch. A nigga did not discriminate.

I stood straight, and we all did some shots that one of my niggas had brought with him. I was feeling hella good as I walked back into the Country Club. I adjusted my pants that were slightly hanging off of my ass and licked my lips. I was getting cotton mouth like a motherfucka. I grabbed me a bottled water and spotted Pia sitting at the table alone looking mad as hell. I chuckled because her ass could have had a million friends if she wanted to she was just so fucking anti-social, but it was cool. She had me, and I was all she needed.

"Bae, why you looking so mean and shit," I said walking to her. My niggas took the empty seats and even pulled another table over to ours. We were deep as hell and smelling like a fucking pound of kush.

"Ahmad, I been sitting her for like ten minutes by my damn self," she complained. Her little pouty ass lip was poked out and everything. I chuckled as I sat down beside her. I leaned my head on her and gazed into her eyes. I swear lately shit been rocky with us, but she was my fucking heart. I wasn't going nowhere, and neither was she.

"I'm sorry. I was getting high baby. You know me," I told her. She rolled her eyes. I leaned over so that I could kiss her lips.

"You are so fucking beautiful, Pia," I told her, meaning it. My baby was the whole package. Mad, angry even crying with that ugly ass face she does she was still a beautiful ass woman to me.

"I mean so fucking pretty. We gotta make a million little girls that look just like you," I told her forgetting that we were surrounded by people. Pia could make me feel like it was just us in a room.

"Yeah and maybe a boy. He gonna be handsome just like you," she said smiling.

"Hell, yeah. I know I'mma have to whoop his little ass, though. I was a bad ass kid, ma," I said, and we both laughed. My eyes landed on that nigga Xerius and I instantly got mad. Fuck was he doing here? I looked at his date and saw he'd brought Rowan's cousin. She was a bad little piece, and I had fucked her a year ago, but she wasn't shit to be pressed about. She was the stuck-up pretty girl type that was really a hoe when she got around a nigga she thought could do something for her. I made eye contact with that nigga, and I mugged him. If he even looked Pia's way, I was gonna fuck his ass up and I didn't give a fuck who was around. His ass had tried me one too many times by constantly contacting her on that hoe shit.

I pulled out a shot and gave it to Pia. She tossed it back, and I leaned in and licked the liquor off of her juicy ass lips. I couldn't wait to eat her pussy.

"Damn…I'm horny," I told her staring into her eyes. She smiled, and her eyes dropped down to my lips.

"I am too baby," she said making me harder.

The DJ started playing "Hot Nigga" and even though it was old that shit still bang. All of my niggas jumped. I grabbed my *right hand*, my baby Pia and made her get with me. I pulled her beautiful ass onto the dance floor and was all in her face rapping. She smiled while doing the hot nigga with me.

Running through these checks 'til I pass out
Your shorty gave me neck 'til I pass out
I swear to God, all I do is cash out
And if you ain't a hoe,

"Get up out my trap house!" Every fucking body yelled. I laughed because my fucking head was spinning and somehow Rowan's ass had come right beside Pia and me. Pia had her back to me, and Rowan was trying to massage my fucking dick. That shit instantly woke a nigga up. I pushed her hand out of the way and before Pia could turn around I started dancing with her while hugging her from the back. The music switched to a slow song, and I hugged her never wanting to let go.

"I love you, baby," I told her and she fell into me more. We swayed with the music until it was time for them to announce the queen and king of the prom.

"Ahmad Matin and Rowan Pitts," the announcer said. I kissed Pia and followed Rowan up to the stage. I put on the crown like the king I was and put Rowan's crown on her. I looked out at the crowd and spotted Pia walking out of the room. I turned to walk away, and Rowan grabbed my hand.

"We gotta dance, daddy," she said, and I pulled her off of the stage. Slow music once again filled the room, and everyone grabbed somebody. I started dancing with Rowan, making sure to not get too close. She gazed into my eyes with watery eyes and I sighed. I wasn't in the mood for her bullshit.

"I remember the first time I saw you. I was riding my bike, and I saw you playing ball with Shyy. I swear you were fine even back then. We instantly clicked, and you liked me too. You always said I was pretty and that one day you would be my man. I think the way you put it was once you get some titties I'll like you," she said, and we both laughed because I did say that shit. I was a wild little nigga for that one.

"Shit you was flat chested as hell," I said chuckling. Rowan frowned.

"I was a damn kid. Your dick wasn't always big," she shot back at me. I stopped dancing and looked at her.

"Cut it out. My shit always been swinging," I said making her laugh.

"No, but for real. It was always us, then you changed. She came along, and you forgot about me. I didn't switch it up. You did," she said as the music changed. Wayne and 2 Chains came on, and Rowan spun around. She was holding her train up by this thing on her wrist. She started working that ass and I made sure Pia was out of the room while she shook that shit. My niggas were surrounding me so you couldn't really see shit, I was doing, but still, I felt nervous as hell. I didn't want my baby wilding out on me.

"You scared of this ass?" Rowan asked, looking back at me. I smirked and slapped her hard on her shit. She made it jiggle some more, and I licked my lips. I looked up, and Pia's fucking ass, like a ghost, was standing in front of Rowan. Rowan tried to stand straight, and Pia snatched her by her hair and slapped the dog shit out of her before punching her repeatedly in the face.

"Damn!" some niggas next to me yelled. I grabbed Rowan and tried to get Pia to let up on her. Pia's beautiful dark brown eyes looked at me.

"You helping this bitch?" she asked, pulling Rowan's hair harder. I immediately shook my head.

"No, baby. I'm just trying to break this shit up," I said and pulled Rowan back again. Pia hit Rowan again, and Rowan tried to slap her back, but I caught her wrist.

"Ahmad, that's not fair! Let her go," Rowan's cousin yelled, running over only to be stopped by my nigga. Rowan's dress was slowly sliding down her body.

"Yeah, let me go! I'mma fuck this hoe up!" she yelled, and I squeezed her wrist tight as hell.

"Aye, watch that shit," I told Rowan. I looked at Pia. "Baby, let her hair go, please," I said as I could see teachers heading our way. I didn't want my fucking wife getting locked up because of this dumb shit. Pia looked at Rowan, and her eyes grew two sizes. She let Rowan's hair go and hocked up a glob of spit and spit in her face. My fucking eyes bugged out at the crazy shit she was doing.

"You're a thirsty ass bitch, and I promise you that no matter what you do he will never love you the way that he loves me," she said and walked off. I let Rowan go as she wiped the spit off of her face. I looked at her and saw my name tatted big as hell on her left breast with a heart going around it along with some roses. I couldn't believe this bitch. I saw the top of that tat outside but not my fucking name. I shook my head and pushed her ass out of the way. I ran like the fucking cops was chasing a nigga out of the room. I caught Pia walking towards the parking lot. I slowed down and took a few deep calming breaths. I knew she was pissed, and truthfully she had every right to be. It was like with Rowan I was toxic, and I couldn't stop myself from fucking up in regards to her. I had to really get a hold on that shit before I lost the love of my life over some pussy.

"Lo siento. Se me sigue jodiendo y prometo hacerlo mejor. Eres el amor de mi vida y que tenías razón. Nunca voy a amar a otra persona el camino te amo. Por favor (I am sorry. I keep screwing around and promise to do better. You are the love of my life, and you were right. I'll never love another person the way I love you. Please)" I begged walking behind her. Because of my love for Pia, I learned Spanish. Pia let me hug her and I took her to the car. We got in, and I sped out of the lot. I took Pia to the room I had reserved for us. While she took off her dress, I ran her a bath and popped some bottles of champagne open. Pia walked past me as I was rolling a blunt and went into the bathroom. My phone buzzed, and I glanced down at it.

Rowan: *So I guess now is as good as any time to tell you I'm pregnant. That's why I got the tattoo. She might have your name but has she given you a baby???*

I quickly erased the message and put my phone away. Rowan was full of shit. I always strapped up. If she was pregnant, it damn sure wasn't by me. I would take that bitch to the clinic my damn self before I let her have my child. Fuck no. Pia would be the only woman doing that. I took off my suit jacket and even my shirt. I turned on Tidal on my phone onto the playlist "*Fuck Pia Silly*" yeah I did shit like that, and I sat back in the chair. I had been fucking up a lot, and I was a little worried that I was losing control of shit. Pia seemed distant as hell, and whenever we were around each other we either argued, or bullshit happened. I was leaving for school in a few months, and Pia had been talking like she wanted to stay here which wasn't a fucking option. If I was going so was she. She could dance anywhere…I shook my head realizing I hadn't seen my baby dance in months. It was like she just stopped going. I got off the bed and went into the bathroom. I stood in the doorway and watched her wash that sexy ass body for me.

"Why did you stop dancing?"

Pia shrugged. Her hair was wet. Her face had been cleaned off that makeup bullshit, and she was looking so fucking pure to me.

"I just did. I see you finally noticed," she replied. I smiled. Didn't she know that slick talk made my dick hard?

"Ma, I know things are rocky with us, but nothing has changed. I still love the fuck out of your ass."

Pia pulled her legs to her chest. The tub was huge and I found myself wanting to get into it on some romance movie type shit, but I didn't. Baths weren't for me.

"Ahmad, your ex has your name tattooed on her chest. The same person I caught you cheating with right before we got married. You told me you were done with her. That I wouldn't have to deal with her thirsty ass for the rest of my life, but she's still here. In the fucking trenches waiting and that's your fault."

I scrunched up my face.

"Fuck you mean that's my fault?"

"Like what the fuck I said! You steady entertaining this fucking girl, and that's why she's fucking hanging on! You don't think people want me, Ahmad? You don't think they're waiting for you to fuck up because they are. The difference between you and me is that you choose to play games with her. I'm not," she said and started putting water all over her body. I was mad as hell at the way she was coming at me. The shit was kind of true, but still. Like her husband, she should have been listening to me and not Rowan's ass.

"Pia, I only want you. I'm married to you. It's always been about you," I said and hit the blunt. Pia nodded. Her fucking attitude was changing by the second. She was gonna have to stop hanging around my aunties and momma. They were making her too fucking defiant.

"We'll see if that's true," she said in this slick ass tone. I walked away not wanting to curse her ass out and went back into the bedroom.

I knew Rowan had fucked up all of my chances at getting my dick sucked, but I could still beat my pussy up so I took off my clothes. I started drinking champagne from the bottle, and ten minutes later Pia walked out of the bathroom. I sat in the chair in nothing but my boxers as she dried off. Pia had these nice ass curves on her body because she was a dancer. I licked my lips eying her body. Whereas Rowan was curvy with a big ass and big titties, Pia was toned with curves. I guess Pia's shape was like a young JLO back when Puff was hitting that shit.

"Dance for me bae.... come dance for daddy," I said and swallowed the lump I had in my throat. The thought of Pia not wanting me made me sick to my fucking stomach. I could be a better husband, and I made a vow to myself to cut

Rowan off for good. No going backs regardless of how Pia and I were doing. That shit was getting crazy and if Pia was to find out the truth I could possibly lose her.

"Ahmad, I'm not really in the mood," she said walking close to me. I kissed her stomach. As always her skin was soft and smelling good. I slowly rolled my tongue around her small belly button. I looked at her in a way that I knew would get her to moving them fucking hips.

"Do it for me…let's enjoy our night…. come on," I begged while slowly rolling my finger through her slippery slit. Pia's eyes closed briefly, and she moaned. She ran her hands through her hair and started to slowly move her body to the beat of the music. I sat back and watched her do her thang. She stared at me, but before I could say anything she turned around. She bent over and grabbed her ankles. She made that ass jiggle, and I pulled my dick out. I put my blunt out and stood. I came closer to her, and she made her ass bounce on my dick. This fucking girl here…I swear she was gonna always be mine. Now if only she could keep this sexy ass persona and slob on my dick, all would be good with us.

"Damn, get on the bed," I said and practically pushed her over to the bed. Pia did as I instructed and climbed her sexy ass on the bed. She got on all fours, and I slapped her ass. I just had to. I kissed both of her ass cheeks and fingered her from the back. She was snug and wet. She started moaning as I pulled my fingers out and slapped the tip of my dick against her opening. I did it a few more times, and she started pushing back begging me to fuck her. I smirked and licked my lips.

"Open my pussy," I said in a low tone. Her fingers moved quickly to my command. I bent down and slowly slide my tongue inside of her. Shit, she tasted so good. She let her lips go, and I pulled back. I slapped her ass hard leaving my hand print.

"Stop playing and keep them open," I said. She opened them back up and I got off the bed. I grabbed my dick and slid into her all of the way hitting bottom. Pia let go and almost fell down.

"Fuck, Ahmad!" she moaned. I smacked her ass and grabbed her hips.

"Pia, you better open my shit and keep it open. You hear me?' I asked and yanked a hand full of her hair. I pulled her head back until she cried out and she held her pussy open for me. I started to rock in and out of her while kissing on her neck. Her pussy was so wet I found myself moaning like a bitch. I sunk my teeth into her skin and she whimpered. She was taking the dick like a good girl, so I knew I had to reward the pussy.

"This pussy feels so good, Pia. I want her to rain on daddy tonight. So you gotta open and let me hit that spot. Okay?"

Pia whined, but she didn't run.

"Okay," she replied in a whisper. I licked my lips. I let her hair go and gripped her ass. I started punishing the pussy.

I was hitting her spot with each thrust making her legs shake. She made this sound and a few minutes later she wet the bed. I rubbed her clitoris to enhance her orgasm.

"Ahmad....shit, fuck, damn!" she cursed coming again. I fucked her harder feeling myself about to nut.

"Pia, suck my nut out…. let me cum in your mouth baby," I said. Just imagining it had me ready to shoot my load off.

"Okay…" she whimpered and I started cumming. I pulled out and she turned around. She grabbed my dick and held out her tongue. I looked down at her as I jacked my shit off on her tongue. My fucking toes curled. My ass was clenched and my balls was tight as hell. Once I was done I fell onto the bed while Pia went into the bathroom. I heard the toilet flush as my dick bricked up again.

"Pia…get my blunt!" I yelled still on my back. She laughed.

"Okay baby," she said. She brought it over lit along with us some water. I smoked as she watched me and I couldn't stop staring at her. She was so fucking gorgeous and I knew that I was fucking her over. I was wrong as fuck for that. Rowan was cool, the pussy was good but it wasn't worth losing my wife. That shit I had with her was dead and that was on my mom's grave.

Chapter Eighteen

Pia

I walked quietly through Ahmad's parent's home. I had been sick as hell from the stomach virus and was in search of some kind of anti-nausea medicine. Sophie usually kept some in the kitchen. I walked down the hall towards the kitchen, and I could hear Sophie talking.

"Ameer, look he's hanging with him daily. You said Tuck is hustling and shit. What if he got Ahmad selling drugs too?" she asked with worry in her voice. I stopped mid-step and listened. I didn't wanna intrude on their talk.

"Baby, I would kill that little nigga and fuck Ahmad up if he ever tried to sell drugs. He's fucking rich. He doesn't have to be a drug dealer. Calm down baby, you're just being paranoid," Ameer replied.

"Nah, I don't trust that little nigga. He looks grimy as hell and kids do stupid shit all of the time, Ameer. Ahmad could be living out some rap song or some shit. You never know. He has all of these questions. He's asking about Tatum more and more. We're gonna have to tell him something," she replied.

"Look, that side of his family ain't shit, and neither was his mother. The bitch helped that nigga kidnap you and do all of that bullshit. She even poisoned her own fucking son. She deserved to fucking die, Sophie. Even though you pulled the trigger I know in my heart that I should have," Ameer said in a cold tone.

"Hmph," I said dropping my phone by accident. Sophie and Ameer walked into the hallway and looked at me. Ameer shook his head and walked away while Sophie stared me down. She walked over to me and grabbed my phone.

"Pia, please come talk with me," she said and walked away. I was so afraid that I started shaking. Slowly, I walked down her hallway and into the family room. They only used the formal living room around the holidays. Sophie sat her cream leather and suede sofa with her eyes on me. I could tell she had been crying, and I really shouldn't have listened to them, but I was trying to be polite and not interrupt them. I had no clue I would hear something so crazy from either of them.

"Okay, Pia, first I have to tell you that what you heard cannot be repeated to your husband," Sophie stopped talking. She wiped her eyes as she looked back at me.

"Ahmad's mother wasn't a good mother. There really isn't any other way to say it. She did a lot of stuff to hurt a lot of people, including Ahmad and me. She poisoned him with Pine-Sol, and because of her, he was taken away from Ameer and me for a while. She helped someone that Ameer was beefing with kidnap and rape me. They did a lot of hurtful things to me, and I almost lost Soraya because of it. What you heard Ameer say is true. I did kill her, and I don't regret it. What I do hate however, is my son being in pain because of it."

"I love Ahmad…." Sophie's beautiful face softened. "I love him so much. From the minute I saw him, I knew that I would always have a special place in my heart for him. He is my son. The truth about his mother can never come out," she said, and I nodded completely understanding. I trusted Sophie and Ameer. If she said his mother was those things, then I believed her. Ahmad's cousin Tuck looked crazy as hell. I could only imagine what type of shit he had planned. It, however, did hurt my heart to hear Ahmad's mother was so ruthless. This was definitely something he should never know.

"Even her brothers, one of which is Tuck's father, were crazy. They tried to kill Erin, Drew, Kasam and one of them shot Quinn. That side of his family is tainted. I don't trust them, and if granny gets out of line, trust she can get it too because I don't play about my son or my family. Ameer and I have worked hard to get him to the point he is at. He's about to play college basketball and get his degree in communications. They will not fuck this up for him. I won't let them. As his wife, it's your job to have his back, Pia. He is the other half of you. Protect him as he would you," she said and leaned over to kiss my cheek. She hugged me gently.

"I promise not to tell," I whispered to her. She pulled back and smiled at me.

"I know you won't," she replied and prepared to walk away. I thought about everything that she had said for a minute before going to find the medicine. I planned on being there for Ahmad as much as I could be, and things had been better since prom. But it was time for us to graduate and I was trying to find a way to tell him that I wasn't going to college with him after all. I knew he would be mad but the more I thought about it. I was choosing myself, and I could go to dance school in Michigan and try to reconnect with my family while he was away focusing on his himself. I missed them and dancing. I felt like Pia Matin was someone I didn't even know.

*****

The next day I walked out the school and bumped into Xerius. I had been purposely avoiding him since prom. Everyone knew about my fight with Rowan. I was embarrassed, to say the least. I had been done with classes, but I still had to pay for my cap and gown. I was coming from lunch with Portia. I had practically begged her to ask my dad to come to the graduation. She said she would, but who knows. All I could do was hope he had a change of heart and decided to show up with my brothers.

"Look at you Sweet P. You looking beautiful as always," he said looking damn good himself.

I smiled. Xerius was tall, toffee colored with brown eyes, thick brows and full lips. He was sexy, and his charming attitude made him a lady's man.

"Thank you Xerius. How have you been?"

He gave me the up and down.

"Good now that I've seen you. Ahmad got you curving a nigga and shit," he replied. We both laughed. I tried to walk past him, and he grabbed my arm. I couldn't help but smell his alluring cologne. Xerius was rocking black from head to toe with his black wood framed Cartier glasses covering his eyes. He pulled me close to him and smiled at me.

"Come ride with a nigga. I mean I know you got Ahmad and trust I'm not trying to step on anyone's toes, but I feel like it's no harm in you having a friend. Come chill with a nigga," he said smiling. I felt like even thinking about it was somehow cheating on my man, but still, I found myself nodding and following Xerius to his black Camaro. He opened the car door for me and as I slid in he chuckled.

"Pia, you just don't know," he said and closed the door. I ignored his little comment and got comfortable in my seat. I texted Jess as he got in and pulled off. I was so nervous. I wasn't going to do anything with him, but I knew if Ahmad was to see us out he would lose his damn mind.

Me: *Hey so do you have male friends?*

Jess*: Ummm actually I do. Why did you ask? You being a bad Pia?*

I laughed.

Me: *No I'm not, but I am chilling with a friend. I'm not doing anything wrong, but still, it feels weird.*

Jess: *I think as long as you're respectful to your marriage you're not doing anything wrong.*

Me: *Thanks! I'm being a good wife. As good as my husband he's to me.*

Jess: *Oh shit….be how you would want him to be with you*

I smiled and put my phone away. Around twenty-five minutes later we pulled into a park. We were in the city and honestly I hadn't ever really been in Detroit like that. I noticed we were around a lot of other Camaros. I assumed he was in a car club or something.

"These my people Pia you good," he said and got out of the car. I slowly got out and pulled down my top. I was wearing light blue wash skinny jeans with a white cami that came down to the top of my jeans. On my feet were some white thong sandals and my hair was a little plain looking today, just straight and pulled back into a ponytail. Compared to how the other girls were dressed I felt way overdressed. I was used to being like that, though. These girls were dressed like how Portia usually dressed. In barely there clothing with their ass hanging out. Looking for attention.

"This my home girl, Pia," Xerius said as we approached a group of people. They were all young and good looking. The women were giving me this stank ass face, but the dudes. The dudes were grinning at me like I was the best thing since sliced bread.

"Pia how you know this nigga?" a tall, dark-skinned guy asked me. I smiled as Xerius grabbed my hand. With me being surrounded by so many people I didn't know I found comfort in his touch.

"Pia, this my cousin Will and his friends. As you can see we love Camaros," he said, and they all laughed. I smiled as I looked around. All of the cars were nice and had some type of freaked out feature on them. Whether it be a grill or rims.

"These are some nice cars," I said, and Xerius took me over to a white Camaro. He opened the back door, and the back seat was filled with all kinds of liquor on the seat. He made himself a drink in a red plastic cup and looked at me. I wasn't in the mood for drinking, so I shook my head, and he gave me a bottled water. He passed his cup my way as he closed the door.

"Take a sip so you can relax. You look uncomfortable as hell girl," he joked. I laughed. Shit, I was. I took a sip and gave the cup back to him. We went back to his car and got in. He let his windows down and turned on his radio. I looked around at all of the people that filled the parking lot.

"So how shit been going with you and Ahmad? That prom shit was wild as hell," he said breaking the silence. I nodded.

"Yeah. I don't usually act like that," I said still embarrassed by my behavior. Ahmad brought out the good and bad in me.

"Shit, you had every right to be pissed but…I mean you should have been whopping his ass too. He should have never been fucking with her like that anyway since y'all married and shit. Ahmad has always been for self, though," he said. I looked at him. It was cool for me to talk about him, but I wasn't about to let some other nigga diss him.

"I know Ahmad better than anyone. I don't need for you to do whatever it is your trying to do. He's my husband," I said with an attitude. Xerius raised his hands in the air.

"My bad. I'm just trying to look out for you. I've always liked you, and I hate to see good girls get the short end of the stick and shit. These hoes be winning," he said chuckling. I smirked, but I didn't have shit to laugh at. Ahmad has promised to do right, and I love him, so I'm staying with him, but I'm not sure anymore what the future is for him and me. I sometimes felt like we were so young and in over our heads, but just the thought of leaving Ahmad damn near gave me a panic attack, so at this point, I wasn't sure what was best for me.

After chilling with Xerius and his family for a few hours, he took me back to my car. It was now dark outside, and I was buzzing a little from sipping on his drink with him. Xerius had been the perfect gentleman, and I enjoyed spending time with him. I didn't think I would do it again to keep the drama at bay, but still I had fun.

"So Pia that was cool. You fun as hell to be around, ma," he said with glazed over eyes. I smiled because he looked so sexy like this. His glasses were now gone, and he had these hooded eyes that were so handsome on him.

"You cool as hell too," I said taking my seat belt off. Xerius sat up and before I registered what he was doing he leaned towards me. He gently kissed my lips. I closed my eyes with my heart beating a mile a minute. He tried to stick his tongue into my mouth, and I lightly shoved him back. He chuckled, staring me down.

"He gone fuck up and I'mma be here waiting. He don't know what he got Pia," he said in a serious tone. I cleared my throat and opened the car door.

"Okay, well you have a good night and drive safe," I said quickly getting my ass out of the car. I went to my car and got in. As I was driving home, my cell phone rang.

"Hello," I said taking the call on my car's Bluetooth.

"Bae, I wanted to come home to pussy and food. Where you at? I need a back massage, and I wanna rub on your booty," Ahmad whined into the phone, making me laugh. His voice alone had me feeling guilty for kissing Xerius back.

"I'm headed home now baby. I was with Jess," I quickly lied.

"Okay, I'mma hop in the shower and pull out some food for you to make for us. Aye, Pia," he said.

"Yes, baby," I replied.

"I love you, and I'm committed to making this work. I promise you that bullshit is over. Hurry home daddy's waiting," he said and ended the call. I continued to drive with Ahmad on my mind. Xerius was cool, sexy as hell, and seemed to be a good guy. But he wasn't Ahmad, and he never would be, so he was wasting his time.

Chapter Nineteen

Ahmad

"Ahmad, what's this?"

I ignored her and tossed that shit onto her lap.

"Go take it," I said and started back looking through Pia's phone. She'd left her shit at home by accident, and I was just making sure she was being a good girl. I didn't see anything out of the way, so I put her phone into my back pocket. I had shit to do, and Rowan was holding me up.

"Ahmad, this is so fucking dumb. I'm pregnant with your child," she said, still sitting down. I glanced at the time and knew she had to speed this shit up.

"Go take that fucking test, now!" I said, grilling her ass. She got off of the bed and did as I said. I was running late for Pia's graduation, and she wanted to play fucking games and shit.

"I can't pee!" she yelled. I stepped off of her dresser and stretched out. I swear this girl was gonna make me bust her fucking head wide open. I walked to her bathroom and spotted her sitting on the toilet with this stank look on her face. I walked in and glanced at myself in the mirror. I was on my shit today for my baby's graduation. I was draped in Tom Ford from head to toe. My pops had my suit custom-made and I had on my black Balmain loafers with my white shirt unbuttoned at the collar. I didn't wanna do a tie and shit, but this was nice. Rowan's sneaky ass eyes were fucking up my day, though.

"Ahmad, you look nice," she said smiling.

I chuckled. *This bitch here.*

"Rowan, off the strength of the love I used to have for you I'm not acting a fool on you, but this is a wrap. You a sneaky ass conniving bitch and I can't play games with you because I'mma been done fucked around and strangled your ass. We both know you not pregnant, so drop that shit now. If you pop up on my doorstep with some bullshit or even start throwing dirt on my name, I'mma have somebody handle your ass," I said and walked away.

I quickly walked out of Rowan's house and slipped into my new car. I pulled off, and my cell phone rang. I answered the call as I sped down the street. I knew that I was gonna be a little late, and I still had to get her flowers to put on her car. Fuck.

"Hey ma, I'm coming," I quickly said.

"Ahmad hurry! She's about to speak," my mom said and ended the call. Pia was the Valedictorian of her senior class. I drove a little faster and stopped by the flower shop that was on the way to the school. After grabbing the biggest bouquet that they had, I did fucking ninety to the school. I parked near the door and jumped out. Quickly, I rushed inside the school. The room the ceremony was being held in was filled with so many damn people. I spotted my peoples taking up two rows and shit. I chuckled at their asses, happy to see they came out for my baby and walked over to them. My mom looked at me and gave me the evil eye before smiling at me. She knew she couldn't stay mad at me for too long.

"Ahmad, where were you at?" Soraya's little-grown ass asked me with her hand on her hip. I chuckled while shaking my head.

"Don't worry about it," I said and ruffled her hair that had been straightened, so it was hanging down her back. She frowned and quickly fixed it. I pulled out my phone and zoomed in so that I could see Pia. She had sat down from her speech, and she was now about to be called to get her diploma. After going through most of the graduating class, they came to my baby. I hit record geeked up like a motherfucka. My baby was doing it.

"Pia Johanna Matin," the announcer called.

"Go Pia!' Ma yelled.

"Get it, baby!" I yelled, and we all clapped being loud and ghetto as hell. We definitely made the most noise. Pia smiled as she took her diploma. I recorded the whole thing and after she sat back down the ceremony quickly ended. We went outside, and I pulled her new truck a royal blue A3 Audi that I'd gotten with some of my money my grandpa had left me. I wanted to get my baby some swagged out shit for real, but my ma was always on me about spending. She talked me into getting the A3, and I liked it because it actually fit my baby.

I sat Pia's flowers down onto the hood of the trunk and leaned against it as she walked out of the school with my family. She had so many flowers that my pops and uncles were carrying her shit for her. She spotted me, and her beautiful face lit up. She rushed over to me, and I pulled her into my arms. She was wearing this form fitting white bandage dress with some white heels, and she was looking sexy as hell. I wouldn't mind seeing my baby on her shit like this more often.

"Congratulations baby, you did it," I whispered in her ear. She smiled as she pulled back to look at me.

"Thank you, baby," she said and kissed me gently on the lips. I kissed her harder and slapped her ass.

"Ahmad," my ma said blocking me and shit.

"Sophie, he married," my pops said as I pulled back from Pia. I chuckled. My pops was always looking out for me. I loved him for that shit.

"Here baby, this is from me. Congrats on graduating," I said and turned her to her new truck. I wrapped my arms around her from the back and bent my head so that I could kiss her on the side of her neck.

"Daddy got you a new truck," I whispered in her ear.

Pia laughed. She let me go and walked over to it. My ma took a few pictures of her as she opened the door and saw that the inside was legit. I watched her smile, and her eyes even watered as she walked back over to me. She grabbed my face with both hands. I felt my heartbeat quicken as I looked down at her.

"Thank you, Ahmad. I love it, but not more than I love you, my king," she said, and I bit down hard on my bottom lip. Pia and her fucking love for me. Shit sometimes it was almost too much to take.

"I love you too my queen," I said and kissed her again.

"Aww Ahmad," my auntie Erin said as they snapped a few more pictures.

*****

Hours later we sat inside of Pia's favorite restaurant in Troy. I was feeling good. My uncle Kasam had snuck me a few shots, and I had dipped off and smoked a blunt in the parking lot. My ma was mad with me, but shit a nigga was practically grown. She had to let that shit go. Her days of telling what to do were now over. Pia was sitting beside me, but she was looking down as hell. My people were talking and kicking it, but she was just staring off at nothing. I leaned towards her and moved some of her hair out of her face.

"Hey, you good?"

She shook her head. A few minutes later she glanced over at me.

"None of my family came. Not even Portia. Did you call my dad like you said you would?" she asked. Fuck! I had completely forgotten because I had a lot of shit going on. She told me that she was gonna kick it with Portia about them coming and for me to reach out to her pops. It was an honest mistake but still that nigga should have known when the graduation was and to come. He was on some real hoe shit.

"Baby I- "

"Just save it," she said and left. I stood, and my pops grabbed my arm. I looked at him with a frown. How the fuck could she be mad at me? I was the one person that had always fucking been there for her.

"Let her cool off. She misses her people, and it's crazy that they could cut her off like that. I'mma call her pops and Portia and see if I can kick it with them. This shit not right," he said and went back to eating his food. I nodded, walked out of the restaurant and found Pia hugging on that nigga Xerius. It was as if I was having an outer body experience. I ran towards them and shoved his arm hard as hell. He quickly let Pia go, and I went in on his bitch ass. That nigga had me on height, because even though I was tall this nigga was a fucking giant, but I was a beast with these hands. My pops and uncles had been beating me up since I was a little nigga.

"Nigga, I told you when I caught with you what it was gonna be," I said punching him in the face. He hit me back in the chin, and Pia screamed.

"Ahmad stop! He was just giving me a hug," she reasoned, making shit worse. I shook off that bullshit she was talking about and went back at that nigga.

"Xay, what the fuck!" some nigga yelled, and somebody grabbed me into a fucking headlock.

"No, get off of him!" Pia screamed, and started hitting the nigga in the head with her shoe.

"Ah, bitch!" he yelled.

"What the fuck is this shit here," I heard my uncle Kasam say.

Pop! Pop!

I was let go immediately, and I took a few deep breaths. My throat was burning like a bitch. I turned around and saw old boy that grabbed me, and that nigga was built like a fucking tank. My uncle stood glaring at the nigga as Pia put her shoes back on.

"Pia, go get everybody," he said, and she looked at me. I gave her a look that made her ass damn near run into the restaurant.

"I would suggest you two niggas leave immediately," my uncle Kasam said and puffed on his blunt. I tried to grab Xerius bitch ass, and my pops grabbed my arm.

"Ahmad, chill. We in the burbs and I know the cops on the way. Let's go," he said in a low tone.

"Who jumped in?" my uncle Aamil asked with his nose flaring. Kasam gave a head nod to the big nigga, and my uncle walked over to him and hit him one time. He passed out before he even hit the ground.

"Damn, nigga. You hit him like you was one of them fucking street fighter characters and shit. You out here upper cutting niggas and shit," my uncle Kadar said making them all laugh. I even chuckled. My pops pulled me away, and I watched Xerius try to wake up whoever the nigga was that helped him fight me.

I got into my car and waited for Pia to slide in. When she did, we sped out of the lot. We rode in silence as I tried to think of the right thing to say to her.

"You…. you fucking…him?" I asked quietly. Just saying the shit had me sick to the stomach.

"No, you know I'm not," she replied back with an attitude. I chuckled.

"Shit, I don't know what the fuck you doing? Every time I turn around you doing some sneak shit with that nigga."

Pia looked at me and laughed.

"Ahmad, I could say the same for you. Rowan is your fucking shadow, and you want to question me about some shit. You cheated on me with that bitch right before we got married!" she yelled, getting upset. She was low key right, but none of that changed the fact that she was too close for comfort with that bitch ass nigga. I didn't trust his ass.

"What I know is that if I find you talking, texting, or hugging that nigga again, it's gone be a fucking problem," I said so fucking serious.

Pia shook her head with her arms crossed over her chest.

"Yeah, okay," she snapped back. Her little slick ass mouth was gone get her ass in trouble. She cleared her throat before talking again. "Maybe we should take a break? We've never had issues like this before. I want us to go back to how it used to be, Ahmad. We didn't use to argue and hurt each other," she said. I immediately shook my head.

"Nah, Pia. Back then we weren't together, so we didn't have these kind of problems. We going through some shit, but we'll be good," I said and cut up the radio. This nigga Bryson Tiller was on, and his song couldn't have come on at a worst fucking time. He was always in his fucking feelings about some shit. The new fucking Drake and shit.

I wanna know how we became so distant girl
The way we fell in love, it was almost instant
I'm tryna find a way around it
Girl tell me how you feel about it
You still love me, that's the way its sounding
Thank God I would have never found this, I doubt it

His lyrics had Pia silently crying and shit. I grabbed her hand and held it until we made it home. Once we got there, I took her straight to the guest house and locked the door so my family couldn't interrupt us. I took her into the bedroom and helped her remove her stuff. I quickly discarded my clothes, and the only noise that you could hear was Pia's sound machine that she used when we went to sleep. It was making this water sound like the water was hitting against the shore and shit. I grabbed Pia's hand and took her to the bed.

She was looking at me with these sad ass eyes, and I was all fucked up because we were so happy together.

We used to be each other's back bone but now all we did was fight. Things had changed, and I was a little confused on how to get shit back to how it should be. What I did know was that Pia and I splitting up was not an option. She was the one for me, and I was the one for her.

"I love you. I promise things will get better. We gotta make this shit work baby," I said getting into the bed. Pia climbed in with me, and I pulled her on top of me. That sweet ass pussy was warm as it sat directly on top of my shit taunting me. I grabbed her face and pulled her down so that I could suck on her lips. Pia moaned, and I started to harden beneath her.

"Put it in," I said against her mouth. Pia nodded and while I was still kissing her she slowly sat down on me. Fuck, I don't think I could ever describe how good it felt to feel the inside of her. Slowly she started to slide up and down me. I know she wanted me to ease up and let her sit up, but I couldn't. I wanted to have my tongue in her mouth while my dick was deep inside of her pussy. What can I say, with my baby I was greedy, I wanted all of her.

"Fuck, you feel so good," I groaned, and she looked me in the eyes. Her tears fell on my face, and we continued to have sex until we both climaxed.

Two days later I pulled up on my cousin Tuck at one of his spots on the west side off of Six Mile. I parked in front of the bungalow style house and got out. He stood on the walkway with a few of his niggas. They seemed cool I just hated the way they stared at me whenever I was around like I was a God or some shit. That shit made me uneasy. I didn't like that thirsty shit. Because I knew how thirsty these niggas could be I drove my car, my old school instead of my pops whips and I had my cards on me instead of cash. No nigga was going to catch me slipping.

"Here go my nigga Ahmad!" some random nigga I had never seen before said that was sitting on the porch. I nodded to that nigga as I walked over to my cousin. We dapped each other up, and he blew cigarette smoke out of his mouth.

"I need to holla at you real quick about some shit," he said and walked off towards my car. I followed him, and we both got in.

"What's up nigga?"

He sighed. He tossed his cigarette out of the window and looked over at me.

"I remember you saying your uncle's pops was the plug and shit."

I chuckled.

"I ain't say no shit like that to you," I said no longer smiling. Fuck type shit was this nigga on. "Matter fact I'mma fuck with you later," I said, starting my car. My cousin sat in his seat.

"Nigga this me. I'm not on snake type shit," he said raising his shirt.

"I lost my plug. My fucking traps were raided, and I lost a lot of money so I couldn't pay the nigga back on time. I borrowed the money from granny, but now because I'm late this nigga good on me. I was thinking that you could come in as a silent partner, and we could both run the D. We'd be legendary, nigga. All we would need is the plug which you got," he said smiling at me. I looked straight ahead. Why the fuck would I give up college basketball for drug dealing?

"Man, you know I fuck with you, but I got some good shit happening in my life right now."

"I know, and that's why I said, silent partner. While you away at school making shit happen I'm here making money for the both of us. You think I would cut you out of the profit?" he asked looking offended.

"No, it's not even about that. This is about me and my life. Nobody tells me how my future should go but me. Ever since I was a child all I wanted to do was play ball."

Tuck laughed.

"Okay nigga, this ain't no Michael Jordan commercial and shit," he cracked. I smirked.

"Nah, but seriously. That shit too easy and I enjoy doing it. I'm not risking that for nobody. That plug shit is dead. I'm sorry but I can't help you, nigga," I said shrugging. He nodded with his jaw all tight and shit. I knew he was mad, but I didn't give a fuck.

"Okay...I guess I can understand that. Well let's go hit up a strip club and check on granny," he said.

"Bet," I said pulling off. Now that we could do.

*****

After kicking it with my family on my mom's side, I went to my uncle Aamil's house. I sat in my car, and my cousin Tuck called me again. I answered and placed the call on speaker. My uncle actually slid into my car as he started talking.

"Man, I just wanted to see where your head was at again with that shit," Tuck said.

My uncle looked over at me as he stretched out in his seat.

"I'm still on that same shit. I'm'a hit you back," I said, ending the call. I had never considered hustling, but Tuck had brought the shit up, so I did have questions. Shit, if basketball didn't work out for me, I could have that to fall back on.

"What's going on?" Aamil said. He pulled a blunt out of his pocket and rolled the window down. He didn't stay too far away from where I lived, and he was like a dad to me shit all of my uncles were, but I knew I couldn't go to my pops with this. He would straight flip out on me.

"Nothing. Just coming back from kicking with my cousin and granny."

My uncle nodded with an irritated look on his face. I did get a little irritated at the way they acted about Tatum and her family. Was she really that fucked up of a person?

"Oh, okay," he said lighting the blunt. He took a few hits before talking to me. "So what's going on?"

"Was she that fucked up of a person?" I asked really wanting to know.

He passed me his blunt.

"She was. She did some shit that was beyond fucked up Ahmad. It's not important just know that we not making shit up about her," he replied. I blew smoke out.

"I know. I trust y'all still I have questions. My pops wanna choke me and shit for just asking about her," I said and laughed even though the shit really wasn't nothing to laugh at.

"You came over here to ask me some questions about your moms?" he asked. I looked over at him while passing the blunt back to him.

"Nah, actually came by to ask about hustling. How is it? I mean if I knew somebody that needed a plug would Mason be the person I could contact?" I asked.

My uncle moved around in his seat. He was my blood, my uncle, shit at the end of the day my mothefucking nigga. I knew he had questions, and I just hoped he didn't go to my pops with the shit we talked about.

"Ahmad," he smiled then chuckled. He tossed the blunt out of the window and sat back. "Ahmad, you not a hustler. You a ball player. You been bouncing balls since before you could fucking talk. That's what you were put here to do," he said. I nodded agreeing with him.

"I know and it's not for me."

Aamil smiled.

"I know. Your thirsty ass cousin trying to get put on already. Nigga just met you and already asking for shit," he said, shaking his head. I sat back and held my tongue. Tuck was cool. It wasn't his fault his pops and uncle were killed. He wasn't given the same opportunities in life that I had been given.

"He cool as hell. Some of his spots got raided and well he asked me if I could talk with Mason."

Aamil cleared his throat.

"Blood don't always mean family. Your grandmother Alana killed your grandpa and helped your mom do some foul ass shit. She tried to put my own fucking brothers against me. Everybody that you show love to is not gonna show you that same love back. That's just real. I know right now you finding yourself and dealing with a lot of shit, but don't ever forget who really got your back."

Aamil smiled at me.

"Shit, I'll go through the trenches with you, Ahmad. You not just Ameer's son, you my son too. If hustling was the only option, then we would be out there making that shit happen, but it's not. So fuck what Tuck talking about and get your degree, along with that championship ring for the D. You and Mauri can be on the court killing some shit," he said and dapped me up. I gave him a quick hug and nodded. He was right. Tuck's situation wasn't mine, and I couldn't fuck up what I had trying to help him out. He was just gonna have to find his own connect.

Chapter Twenty

Pia

Xerius: *I know shit complicated with me and your nigga, but I miss talking to your beautiful ass. Can you at least text me?*

Xerius: *hit me back sweet p…*

I put my phone away and looked around the room. I was out of breath and tired, but damn it felt good to be back in dance class. I had been in dancing school since I was a child. I started out in ballet, but I knew how to do all types of dancing. For the moment I was feeling hip hop and had been doing some choreography with some great dancers. My ultimate dream was to have my own dance school. Dancing gave me this feeling that I couldn't explain. It also reminded me of the good times I shared with my dad.

"Pia, that was so good. Look, I have some things coming up, and I would love for you to try out. You should come out," the choreographer said and walked away. I smiled so hard it stretched my face. I walked out of the building and spotted Rowan leaning against my car. Ahmad and I had been good since my graduation. He had been busy with basketball, but still things with us were much better. I had no clue what this hoe wanted, and I was in no mood to play games with her.

"What the fuck you want?" I asked popping my trunk so that I could toss my bag into it. Rowan stepped off of the car and smiled. She looked like her usual self, cute but slutty mixed in with a lot whole bunch of hoeness.

"Pia, I won't be long. I've been so torn on what to do," she said and touched her forehead. This bitch was so extra. "I mean, I don't like you, I never have. You're not as cute as me, and your style is nonexistent, but still he married you. He claimed to love you more," she said. I placed my hand on my hips.

"It wasn't a claim. Bitch, he does love me more. When he let me whoop your ass at the prom, he showed you he loved me more. When he asked me to marry him, he showed you he loved me more. What more do he gotta do for your stupid ass to get that?"

Rowan smiled, but her eyes. Her eyes told the truth. She was hurt like a motherfucka at my words.

"Well since he loves you so much, tell me how come I'm about to have his baby," she said and handed me her phone. On it was a recording. I clicked on it, and Ahmad's face popped onto the screen, and I saw they were face timing.

"Ahmad, a test isn't necessary. We both know I'm pregnant by you," Rowan said to him.

Ahmad looked like he was in his car.

"Rowan, every time I'm in that shit I'm strapped up. You taking that fucking pregnancy test because I don't trust your ass and even if you are, it's not my baby," he said, breaking my heart with just a few words.

"Ahmad, we should be getting ready for graduation. Look I gotta go," she said and the video ended. Rowan looked at me with a satisfied smirk on her face. I dropped her phone onto the ground and stomped the screen off of that bitch.

"You bitch!"" Rowan yelled and pushed me into my car. I lunged at her and slapped her so hard her eyes watered. She jumped back and threw her hands in the air.

"I'm pregnant! Help! She's attacking me! Attempted murder!" she yelled. A few people walking in the parking lot looked at us, including my choreographer. I jumped in my car and sped off, not waiting for them to walk over. Just thinking of Ahmad fucking that hoe when we were married brought tears to my eyes. I cried as I pulled onto the freeway. I quickly drove to the house. I parked behind Sophie and got out of the car. I ran to the guest house and rushed to the bedroom. I pulled out all of my suitcases and started tossing my stuff into them.

"Pia, can you watch Ameerah while I run Soraya to the hospital. She has a high fever," Sophie said walking into the room.

She looked at the mess of the room then back at me.

"What's going on baby?" she asked leaning against the door.

I looked at her, and I just broke down even more. She walked over to me and pulled me into her arms. I cried for a minute before letting her go. She turned to me with concerned eyes.

"Pia, just calm down. What's going on?" she asked again.

I wiped my eyes. I pulled my hair at the scalp because I honestly felt like I was about to go fucking insane.

"Ma…he cheated on me again with her. She showed me this video of them talking about her possibly being pregnant right before his graduation," I was finally able to let out. Sophie's face fell. She shook her head. I could tell she was hurting for me.

"Pia…. I'm sorry this happened. Counseling could help. You're both young and giving up on your marriage shouldn't be the first thing you think of. Ahmad loves you, and I know you love him," she replied. I shook my head while continuing to toss stuff into the suitcase. "If I was Soraya and she was with someone that cheated on her before her wedding then after, what would you tell her to do?" I asked.

"Leave him," Sophie said, without having to even think about it.

"I have to do this, ma. He's not the same. Things had been better, but still, I could feel the end was near with us. He's even considering selling drugs with his cousin. I heard him telling Shyy about it on the phone this morning when he thought I was asleep. The Ahmad I loved would never do me like this or keep all of these secrets," I said zipping my case.

"Pia," Sophie sighed. "This is too much. Ahmad isn't doing shit with that boy. He's nothing just like Tatum or those trashy ass people," she said with a disgusted look on her face.

"Damn, Ma tell me how you really feel," Ahmad said, stepping into the room holding flowers. He dropped them onto the dresser along with his car keys. "I mean that trash did help create me. So what am I trash too?" he asked. Sophie immediately shook her head no.

"Sophie we gotta go," Ameer said walking into the room. He looked at the stand-off between Sophie and Ahmad and his brows furrowed. "What's wrong?"

"I walk in on ma calling my family trash and shit like they blood not fucking running through me," Ahmad replied. Ameer glared at him.

"Watch your fucking tone, Ahmad. Those motherfuckas is no good. They not shit. The only good thing Tatum ever did was create you," he replied with such malice in his voice. I walked over to Ahmad and touched his arm. I could see things getting really out of hand.

"Damn, so it's fuck them, huh? You got that much hate for them…I mean enough to kill 'em? Enough to wrap the woman that created me in a fucking blanket all dead and battered like she wasn't shit. You hated her that fucking much?" he asked. I hugged his arm. Yes, he'd pissed me off, and I was so done with him it wasn't even funny, but still, this moment didn't need to happen ever. Sophie and Ameer loved him so much. Why couldn't he see that?

"Ahmad, them niggas not shit. Your fucking granny ain't shit, and neither is that wanna be hustling ass cousin of yours. I tried to spare your feelings, but if you wanna take it there we can," he said looking Ahmad in the eyes. Sophie walked over to Ameer with her tears falling from her eyes. She whispered something to Ameer, and he shook his head. "Nah, he wanna pop off like them niggas done did some shit for him when I been the one raising him even when his bitch ass momma was alive," Ameer replied angrily. Ahmad tried to move, and I hugged him so tight it hurt.

"Ahmad, please calm down," I said to him.

"Nah, Pia, fuck this nigga. You wanna talk about Tatum like that when she fucking dead and gone? You's a bitch ass nigga for that shit for real. I didn't wanna believe that you would do that shit, but I do now. You hate them that much. What could she have possibly done for you to wanna kill her? Huh, nigga?" Ahmad asked with his skin flushed from being angry.

Ameer went to talk, and Sophie looked at Ahmad.

"Ahmad, I killed your mother," she said, and it was like all of the air was sucked out of the room.

To be continued…

CPSIA information can be obtained
at www.ICGtesting.com
Printed in the USA
LVOW04s1533290916
506737LV00014B/1034/P